ABOUT THE AUTHOR

Jenny Ford is a mum, author and Co-Presenter on her local radio station in Hertfordshire.

In 2010, Jenny discovered that she had MS which was life changing for her. From running her own successful business as a beauty therapist, she had no choice but to give it up. Times were pretty tough for Jenny. Her once happy, busy life had now turned into misery and depression. Family and friends were great, but Jenny felt very much alone.

Then in 2014, Jenny had a spiritual re-awakening, rediscovering her faith. Through prayer and being introduced to meditation, she was given an amazing blessing and a new passion - writing! This was more of a surprise to Jenny than anyone as she had no interest in writing at all, not even as a child. With this new lease of life things started to look up for the first time in years. Not only had she been blessed with this new career, but in 2015 Jenny had the opportunity to become a Co-Presenter on her local radio station. Life began to feel exciting again!

We may go through many challenges and sufferings in life, but things can turn around. Jenny's condition may remain the same, and yes she has bad days, but her way of thinking has changed!

"Just have faith, trust and belief in yourself, look how life amazingly changed for me!"

Visit her website: jennyfordbooks.com

Never let fear stand
in the way of your
dreams!

Jenny

GABRIELLA'S TRAVELS

ISBN: 9781849149082

Published by CompletelyNovel.com

First published in the UK in 2015 by
CompletelyNovel.com

Printed in the UK by Lightening Source

Cover credited to Dreamstime

Gabriella's Travels

By Jenny Ford

Completelynovel.com

ALSO BY JENNY FORD

A Collection of Inspirational Guided Prayers.

Prisoner Within.

1

The Rossini family live in a beautiful picturesque town called Positano, situated in the Campania region of Italy on the Amalfi coast where they own a small patisserie. There was Mama Rosa and papa Joe and their four children, Anthony and Mario who were both married. Michael, and their youngest and only daughter Gabriella. The Rossini patisserie was well known for its delicious pastries that had been passed down through generations of Rossini's using only the finest ingredients. The taste and textures of the pastries were divine. People would come from nearby towns to purchase them.

All four children helped in the patisserie, Anthony who was the eldest and Mario the second eldest helped papa make the pastries and Michael and Gabriella helped mama out front. Michael was heading off to Paris soon to finish his last year training to be a chef, his dream was to one day own his own restaurant and be one of the greatest chefs in Italy. He loved working at the patisserie and helped his parents out every time he came home. He had learnt a lot from his father but it's not where he wanted his career to be.

Gabriella was eighteen and just left school, she was quite a determined girl and knew what she wanted. Ever since she was a little girl she would say to her family "when I'm old enough I want to travel all around Europe and explore all the different cultures." Her family would laugh.

"No Bella" papa would say. "You will work here in the family business, this will all be yours one day."

I'll be an old lady by the time that happens she thought to herself. I will go to Europe, I will save every euro I get. And that is exactly what she did.

Gabriella's parents started to pay her for working in the patisserie when she was twelve years old. It was only a few euros but as she got older the money went up, and was paid even more in the high season when it got really busy. She also did extra work in the evenings helping students with their English language as Gabriella's English was excellent.

In her spare time Gabriella would study the map of Europe and mark off all the places she wanted to visit.

"Gabby you're not really going to do it?" her friends would say.

"Of course I am, I want to travel before I get married so I can then tell my children about all the wonderful exciting places I have seen."

"Your parents will go mad!" added Maria. Maria was Gabriella's best friend, they had known each other ever since kindergarten.

"I know" replied Gabriella "but by the time I'm twenty I would have saved enough money and then I'm off."

Gabriella worked hard at the patisserie working all the hours that she could. She would fit in as many English classes just so she could earn extra money for her travels.

It was the weekend, and Maria came to see Gabriella.

"Hey let's go to the cinema? There is a really funny film on."

"I don't feel like it," sighed Gabriella.

"Come on, you need to have a bit of fun, you work all hours, you need to let your hair down."

"I would prefer to just stay here and do something."

"Gabby it's not going to make a huge difference to your bank balance!" Maria joked sarcastically.

"I know; I just don't feel like going to the cinema."

"You really are serious about this travelling?" addressed Maria.

"You know I am."

"Well we have to do something? Let's meet the others down at the lakes."

"Okay."

The lakes were beautiful, especially in the summer. This was the local gathering place where they could swim and it was free! All of Gabriella's friends knew of her travelling plans, some of them would tease her about it, but that's only because they were envious, then others were very excited for her.

"I wish I had your confidence to travel alone" exclaimed Angelica. "Are you not scared?"

"No not at all I can't wait to go. Just one more year."

"Gabby! Angelica! Come on its lovely in here," shouted Maria.

It was an extremely hot day so the water was very inviting and refreshing.

"What are you going to wear for your party tomorrow," asked Maria?

"I'm not sure yet, something very glamorous!" laughed Gabriella.

And with that they enjoyed the rest of the day having fun at the lakes.

Next morning Gabriella woke up full of excitement, mama and papa were organising a gathering with family and friends for Gabriella's birthday. Papa made a beautiful cake with lots of lovely different fruits, and mama made salads, pasta dishes and prepared different kinds of meat, and of course some yummy Rossini pastries. Gabriella loved family gatherings especially birthday ones!

"Morning Gabriella," said mama and papa. "Happy birthday Bella," they said, giving her a big hug. "Now what would the birthday girl like for breakfast?"

"Ooh, pancakes and blueberries please with a glass of freshly squeezed orange."

"Coming right up. So, what are you going to do today whilst we get prepared for your party?"

"I am going to meet my friends for a milkshake and just hang out."

"That sounds nice, please make sure you are back in time to get ready for your party."

"I will," replied Gabriella as she went to get ready. "Thank you for the lovely breakfast." She kissed her mother goodbye.

Gabriella met her friends at café shake.

"Happy Birthday Gabby!" shouted her friends.

"Thanks everyone."

"So what did you get?" asked Marco.

"Don't be so rude," replied Angelica.

"What! I only asked what she got for her birthday, what's wrong with that?"

They all laughed.

"I don't know yet," beamed Gabriella, "I get them tonight."

"Well, we have all chipped in," smiled Angelica, "it's not a lot but we thought it could go towards you're travelling funds." She gave Gabriella 80 euros.

"Guys, thank you so much, that will help a lot."

"Just one year to go," added Maria. "Have you planned where you want to go?"

"I have, I will tell you nearer the time. Let's enjoy today and look forward to tonight!"

***

"Gabriella are you nearly ready? Your guests will be here soon."

"Yes I'm coming."

Gabriella wore a lovely sky blue halter neck dress that just passed her knees, white flat shoes and accessories. She felt very glamorous.

"Gabriella you look beautiful," beamed her proud parents.

"Thank you. I feel beautiful."

The guests started to arrive, wishing Gabriella a happy birthday.

"Grazie," she replied.

 The Rossini's were a big family there were so many uncles, aunts, cousins. It took a while to greet everyone, then all of Gabriella's friends started to arrive.

"You look great Gabby."

"Thank you, you all look great too."

"Wow there are so many people here," remarked Angelica.

"I know. My parents invite the whole family to everything!" she said smiling.

The evening was going really well. There was a lot to eat and drink, some of the uncles were entertaining everyone with music and songs, which got people up and dancing. Everyone was having a great time, especially Gabriella.

"Can I have your attention everyone," announced papa. "First, I would like to thank everyone for coming to celebrate our little bambino's birthday."

"Papa!" sighed an embarrassed Gabriella.

"Sorry, I mean our very grown up beautiful daughter." Everyone laughed. "And for all of your kind gifts. I would like you all to raise your glass to Gabriella."

"To Gabriella."

"Now bring in the cake!"

It was a very big cake made with lots of lovely fresh fruit. It took two people to carry it. As the cake was being brought in Gabriella screamed. It was being carried by her brother Michael who had flown in especially from Paris. As he put the cake down Gabriella ran and threw her arms around him.

"What are you doing here?"

"I wouldn't have missed your birthday sis, plus mama and papa would never forgive me!"

They both laughed. Everyone clapped and cheered, there were tears as well, as the family came to hug Michael.

The evening continued for a few more hours then the guests started leaving. Gabriella said her goodbyes and thanked everyone for coming.

"See you tomorrow Gabby, thanks for a great night," said her friends, each giving her a big hug.

"Phew," yawned Gabriella as she flopped into the chair. "I'm exhausted."

"Did you have a good time Bella?"

"The best."

The main family were still there, it was a Rossini tradition that all the children and their families stay for the opening of the presents. The first present was from her brother Anthony. It was Gabriella's favourite, and very expensive perfume. Mario's gift was a store card to a designer clothes shop. A beautiful necklace from Michael and two hundred euros from her parents. Plus all the other presents from family and friends.

"Thank you all so much, I have had a wonderful evening I love you all."

Anthony, Mario and their families left. Mama and papa started to clear away the mess.

"Leave that," ordered Michael, "Gabriella and I will do it. Go and rest."

"Grazie, we are quite tired." They kissed Gabriella and Michael goodnight.

"Why didn't you tell me you were coming home?"

"Well if I had told you then it wouldn't have been a surprise!" Michael exclaimed, playfully hitting her.

"I've missed you Michael, how long are you staying for?"

"Just a few days, I have to get back to work."

"How are things in Paris?"

"You would love it there Gabby, it's such a beautiful city, the people are great and the food is sooo good!"

"Don't let mama and papa hear you say that, there's nothing better than Italian food!" They both laughed. "So when do you think you will have your own restaurant?

"Not for a while yet, I need to finish my training, then we will see what happens."

"Do you think you will come back?"

"I'm not sure, I do love it in Paris. I have a good part time job working in a top class restaurant, lots of friends. It would be hard to leave."

"Mama and papa will not be happy!" stated Gabriella.

"I know, but it's my life and I have to do what's right for me, just like you do!"

"They are going to go mad when I tell them I'm off travelling next year."

"Well I suggest you start telling them soon so they get used to it," encouraged Michael. "I can tell you all of the best places to visit when you go to Paris."

"I'm so glad you're home Michael, even if it is for only a few days."

***

The birthday celebrations came to an end and Michael had gone back to Paris. Gabriella started planning her travels. Even though it was still a year away, she wanted to get organised. Now for the hard part, how to tell her parents!

She started to leave brochures of different cities in Europe around the house, she left them in the kitchen, the lounge, even the bathroom, but mama would just tidy them away with everything else. Hmm that don't seem to be working she thought. I need to try something else. She phoned Maria.

"What can I do? They don't seem to be getting it."

"Why don't you just tell them," commented Maria.

"Are you mad!? They will go totally crazy, look how they were when Michael told them he was going to Paris to study to become a chef? I'll be going from one country to another by myself. No, it needs to be done in stages."

"Well good luck with that one," laughed Maria.

***

The year was passing by quickly, and the patisserie was as busy as ever. Gabriella was asked to tutor more students in

English which was great, lots more money towards her travels, but still she had not told her parents. "Right they have not got the hint so I guess I will have to tell them." But each time she went to say something Gabriella would chicken out! Come on Gabriella pull yourself together she said to herself. Tonight, I'll do it tonight!

When the patisserie had closed for the day Gabriella made a cup of tea for her parents.

"Thank you Bella, it's good to sit down, it has been a long, busy day."

"Mama, papa I need to talk to you." Here goes, she thought.

"What's wrong Bella?"

"Well do you remember when I was little and I use to say that one day I wanted to travel around Europe?"

"Yes," laughed papa, "just a silly phase you went through."

Oh my god, this is harder than I thought, she said to herself. "Well I still feel like that. I've been saving my money since I can remember and now I have enough saved and I am going travelling next year once I turn twenty."

Her parents just looked at each other in silence. Gabriella sat there holding her breath waiting for their reaction, but nothing.

"I'm really tired," announced mama "think I'll go to bed."

"Me too," said papa, we have an early start in the morning."

"But it's still early!" blurted Gabriella.

"Goodnight Bella."

Gabriella sat there not quite sure what had just happened, maybe they need to sleep on it she thought.

When Gabriella got up the next morning her parents had already left for work. Now normally Gabriella would go with them, so the fact that they did not wait for her meant they were still upset.

Well they can't avoid me forever, she thought, I'll see them at the patisserie.

When Gabriella arrived at the patisserie it was like nothing had happened.

"Gabriella, customers need serving," mentioned mama, not even looking at her.

I'll speak to them later, thought Gabriella.

It had been another busy day, mama and papa hardly said a word to Gabriella it was awful. They were all tired, mama cooked dinner and Gabriella washed up, and still her parents didn't speak to her.

"This is silly," Gabriella pointed out to her parents. "We need to talk about this."

"What are you talking about?" replied papa

"You know exactly what I'm talking about! I know you don't approve of me wanting to travel, but it is something I have always wanted to do, and I want to do it before I settle down, it will be a wonderful experience."

"It may be a wonderful experience for you whilst your mama and I sit here day after day worrying about you, and if you are safe. You are a young women travelling alone. How do you expect us not to be concerned?"

"I understand that you are worried, but I will be fine."

"So where will you stay?"

"In hostels."

"Hostels!" papa shrieked throwing his hands in the air.

"Yes, it will all be organised by a tour company before I go, it will be completely safe. There will be lots of other people going."

Mama started to cry.

"Look what you have done, you're breaking your mama's heart."

"I'm really sorry you're upset," acknowledged Gabriella "but I am going, and I would like to go knowing I have your blessing."

"Never," blurted papa.

Gabriella just looked at him and walked away.

***

Things were not very good at the Rossini's, Gabriella's parents would hardly speak to her. She went to see Maria.

"It went well then?" joked Maria.

"Don't," huffed Gabriella, "it was awful. You would have thought I had committed some terrible crime!"

"Well in their eyes you have."

"Really! I'm nearly twenty, old enough to make my own choices."

"Gabby you are an only daughter of two very catholic, stuck in their way Italians, what do you expect, family is very important."

"I know what you're saying Maria but I expect them to be a bit more understanding."

"Give it time," advised Maria, "there's still six months, I'm sure they will come around?"

"I won't hold my breath!"

2

Gabriella's parents were still not happy about her travel plans.

"Don't worry," papa would say to mama, "Gabriella won't go; it is just another one of her silly phases just like when she was a little girl."

But it was no silly phase. It was time for Gabriella to start booking her trip. Only six months to go. Her first stop would be the UK, then Spain, Madeira, Greece, Malta, Germany, then France. She booked it through an organised tour guide company, all accommodation and tours were booked. Feeling very excited Gabriella called Maria.

"I've done it."

"Done what?" said Maria.

"I've booked my trip."

"No way."

"Yes, I leave the day after my birthday."

"Have you told your parents?"

"Not yet! They're still not really talking to me."

"Oh Gabby, make peace with them before you go."

"I've tried Maria, but they are so stubborn."

"They are not stubborn, well maybe a bit! They just worry about you."

Gabriella tried to find the right moment to approach her parents again, not that there was ever going to be a right moment.

"This needs to be sorted out," Gabriella remarked to her parents. "Why won't you give me your blessing and be happy for me?"

"You are too young to be travelling alone" exclaimed her father.

"I'm nearly twenty, old enough to make my own decisions."

"Well, if that's how you feel Gabriella then there's nothing left to say!" snapped mama.

"I'm sorry you feel like that, but I have already booked it and I leave the day after my birthday."

Her parents looked at her with tears in their eyes.

Gabriella felt really bad that she had upset her parents. Why can't they just be happy for me? She didn't want to leave things like this so she went to see her brother, Anthony, who only lived round the corner.

"Hi sis, what brings you here?"

"Mama and papa. They make me so angry."

"What have they done now?"

"They are so unreasonable, all I want is for them to be happy that I'm going travelling, seeing a bit of the world whilst I'm still young."

"They are just worried about you, you are nineteen, nearly twenty and going alone."

"You sound just like them!"

"Gabriella, I'm a parent and I know that if Sophia wanted to do what you are doing I would be concerned as well. You're their baby, their only daughter, I guess they feel now you are all grown up and independent you won't need them anymore."

"But that's daft, I will always need them."

"So tell them!" encouraged Anthony.

"Thank you big brother, I knew I could count on your advice."

"Any time sis, just don't be too hard on them." He gave her a big hug.

When Gabriella arrived home mama and papa were sitting at the kitchen table having a cup of tea, they looked so sad.

"Would you like some tea, Bella?" asked mama.

"Yes please, but first I want to say that I am really sorry that I upset you both and for the way I spoke to you. That was disrespectful of me. It's just I have been waiting so long to be able to do this, it's a dream I have had for a very long time and I guess I was hoping you would be happy for me."

"Bella, your mama and I have been talking. I won't say that we are happy about it but if that's what you really want to do then you have our blessing."

"Really?"

"Really," replied papa.

"Thank you, you don't know how much that means to me."

Gabriella threw her arms around her parents and gave them the biggest hug.

"The time will go quickly and before you know it I'll be back home making a mess in my bedroom, with you shouting at me to tidy it up!" They all laughed. "I love you both so much."

"We love you too Bella."

***

As the weeks and months went by, Gabriella was very busy working at the patisserie, teaching English and getting everything organised for her trip. Maria came to see if she could be of any help.

"Only two weeks to go?" affirmed Maria. "How are you feeling?"

"Really excited."

"How are your parents about it now?"

"Still not happy but at least we can talk about it without any arguments!"

"Thank goodness for that," smiled Maria. "I'm really going to miss you."

"I'll miss you too. As I told my parents, it will go quickly, and I'll be back before you know it."

***

It was Gabriella's 20th birthday, and the day before her long awaited trip. Mama and papa decided that this time they would have a quiet birthday celebration, just the immediate family.

"I'm just going to go and see Maria and the gang to say my goodbyes. I'll be a few hours."

"Okay," said mama, "see you later."

Gabriella called round for Maria then they went down to the lakes to meet the rest of their friends. When they arrived, all of Gabriella's friends had arranged a surprise birthday come leaving party for her. They had laid out tables with food and drinks, with little flags of all the countries Gabriella would be visiting, there was music and decorations and a big banner saying 'Bon Voyage'. Gabriella looked at Maria with tears in her eyes.

"You knew about this?"

"Of course I did," chuckled Maria, "you didn't think we would have let you go without a proper goodbye do you?"

Everyone gathered around Gabriella asking lots of questions about her trip.

"Do you think you'll come back?" enquired Angelica.

"Of course she will," responded Maria. "You will, won't you?"

"How could I stay away from you lot," laughed Gabriella.

"We thought you might need some help with the different languages, so we got you some phrase books, pens and pads so you can write to us all, and a small teddy bear so that each night when you go to sleep you will know that we are all thinking of you."

Gabriella stood there with tears running down her face.

"You are the best friends that anyone could wish for."

"Group hug!" shouted Marco as they carried on with the party.

After several hours with her friends it was time for Gabriella to go home to her family.

"Thank you so much everyone for a lovely party and my presents. I will write, but seeing as there are too many of you, I will write one big letter and send it to Maria so she can read it to you all."

After lots of hugs and tears Gabriella and Maria left.

When they had reached Gabriella's house she invited Maria in to be with her and the family.

"I won't," said Maria. "You need this time to be with your family."

"But you are a part of my family, the sister I never had."

"I know, but I would rather say my goodbyes just the two of us." The two girls hugged each other for a long time and did lots of crying.

"I'm going to miss you so much" sobbed Gabriella.

"Me too. Promise you will write to me lots?"

"I promise."

"Have a safe journey Gabby, love you lots."

"Love you too."

"Are you okay?" asked Mario as Gabriella walked in. He could see that she had been crying.

"I think so. I'm just being silly."

"Mama has made your favourite meal. Meatballs with spaghetti and mamas homemade sauce, followed by papas cannoli's."

"Sounds good," she said with a smile.

Gabriella's birthday meal was not the same as normal. Usually with every Rossini celebration there would be all the family, uncles, aunts, friends, but this year was very quiet it just didn't feel right, plus her brother Michael was unable to be there.

"You have hardly touched your meal Bella, are you feeling okay?"

"I'm fine mama, just a bit tired."

After dinner was finished, the plates were cleared and washed then they all sat down for present time.

Mario got Gabriella a top of the range camera so she could take lots of lovely photos, from Anthony a new heavy duty rucksack, mama and papa gave her money as they normally did for her birthday but a bit extra this time plus a chain with a guardian angel attached to it to keep Gabriella safe on her travels. There were lots of birthday cards with prayers of protection for Gabriella's journey and lots and lots of Euros. But there was one card missing, from her brother Michael.

"Thank you everyone for your generous gifts."

"I almost forgot," announced papa as he handed an envelope to Gabriella.

As Gabriella opened the envelope she could see it was from her brother Michael, she read it out to everyone.

"To my beautiful Gabby. Sorry I could not be there today, but I am sending you all my love and hugs. Hope you have an amazing adventure on your travels and can't wait to see you when you get to Paris. Your ever loving brother, Chef Rossini!"

Gabriella look at her parents and brothers with her mouth wide opened and tears in her eyes.

"Am I reading this right? Did Michael say Chef Rossini?"

"Yes Bella, your brother is now a qualified Chef! He can now come back home and open his own restaurant here in Italy."

Gabriella was so happy; she couldn't wait until she saw Michael in Paris so she could hear about all of his plans.

"I think I am going to go to bed now if you don't mind, I need to be up early. Thank you all again for a lovely birthday." She hugged them all goodnight, taking Michaels card with her. Gabriella lay in bed thinking about her trip too excited to sleep, eventually she drifted off.

***

Morning had arrived and time for Gabriella's journey to begin.

"Have you packed everything? Do you have enough underwear?"

"Mama" laughed Gabriella.

"Well you can never have enough, I won't be there to do your washing!"

"I have enough!"

"Come and eat, I have made you a big breakfast, you have a long day ahead."

"I'll be down in a minute, just a few last bits to pack." Gabriella took a last look around her room. "See you in several months, room."

The plan was to spend a few weeks in each country, but who knows what would happen!

"Bella!" shouted mama, "your brothers are here to take you to the airport."

"Coming."

After a rushed breakfast it was time to leave.

"Now, I've put some food in your bag in case you get hungry," added mama, trying not to cry.

"Thank you."

"Time to go" said Anthony.

"Well this is it then."

"Anthony, Mario, make sure your sister gets on the plane safely."

"I'm going to miss you" Gabriella told her parents.

"Not as much as we will miss you Bella." They all started to cry.

"Call us when you get to England, and remember to go to church!"

"I will, love you."

So off Gabriella went to start her exciting adventures!

3

Gabriella's first stop was to the United Kingdom. Once they had landed she went to collect her bags, then to find the tour guides. There were about twenty other people on the tour.

"Hi everyone, my name is Susan and this is Mark, Clare and Thomas, we will be your tour guides throughout your trip here in the UK and the other European countries you will be visiting. I will give everyone their agenda once we are on the coach. Does anybody have any questions before we leave?"

"Yes" said one of the party. "Where are the toilets?" Everyone laughed.

"Just over in the corner," Susan smiled. Once everyone had finished, they boarded their coach to take them to London. Gabriella was feeling very excited. I can't believe I'm actually here, she said to herself.

After about a two-and-a-half-hour journey they came to their destination. "Well ladies and gents, welcome to London" said Thomas. "This is where we will be staying whilst you are here." They all got off of the coach and went into the hostel. "There will be four to a room, men and women separate unless you are a couple." We will let you settle in, then go for a walk around so you can get familiar with your surroundings then grab something to eat."

First thing Gabriella did was call her parents.

"Ciao mama."

"Papa quick it's Gabriella!" she could hear her mama say. "Bella, are you okay?"

"I'm fine mama?" she laughed. "We have just got to the hostel and then we are going to have a look around and have something to eat. I just wanted you to know I arrived safely."

"Oh Bella we do miss you."

"Mama, I have only been gone a few hours!"

"I know, but it seems like days Bella."

"Mama I have to go now, I will call you again soon. Give my love to everyone."

"We love you too. Ciao Bella."

Gabriella went to see what room she was in. She was sharing with three other girls. They all introduced themselves. There was Ingrid from Sweden. Ingrid liked to complain a lot, a bit of a drama queen but very funny with it. Martha from Norway. Martha was sensible and serious. And Petra from Australia. Petra was the informative one.

"Hi, I'm Gabriella, nice to meet you all." Gabriella was determined, sensitive and loving.

"I am really looking forward to our adventure together," said Petra, "it's so exciting. How about you Ingrid, is this your first time to London?"

"No, I came here when I was six, not that I really remember it, except that it was always raining! How about you Martha?"

"My father visit's here a lot for his work, but it's the first time here for me. Gabriella have you been here before?"

"No, but I have been dreaming of this day for a very long time, not just being in London but travelling Europe."

The girls were settling in to their room and getting to know each other.

Knock, knock.

"How are we doing ladies?" enquired Clare one of the tour guides. "Just to let you know we will be heading out for dinner in about half an hour, then having a look around so you can get familiar with the area."

"How exiting," added Petra.

They all gathered outside the hostel.

"Okay ladies and gents, the area that we are in is called London Bridge. It is quite central to lots of places and easy to get around on the tubes and buses."

"What's a tube?" asked one of the traveller's.

"Sorry" said Thomas the guide. "A tube is an underground train, they will pretty much get you anywhere in London. I will be giving you all a map of the tubes and buses to help you when you go out by yourselves, plus a guide sheet of places to visit that aren't included on our tour, like shopping areas, churches, that sort of thing. There is a restaurant about a ten minute walk that caters for lots of different food, so there should be something suitable for you all. As there are so many of us I ask you all to try and keep close together, we wouldn't want to lose anyone on their first day! It is a very large restaurant so there should not be any problem fitting all of us in."

After a few hours at the restaurant it was time to head back to the hostel. Most people managed to introduce themselves to each other.

"Right folks, it's been a long day for everyone!" exclaimed Mark, another one of the guides. We have an early start in the morning for our first visit, which will be a boat trip on the Thames and then a ride on the London Eye. We will give you a wakeup call at seven thirty for breakfast and then we will aim to set off at around nine thirty. I hope you all have a good night's sleep. See you bright and early in the morning."

Gabriella, Petra, Martha and Ingrid headed back to their room. "I am exhausted," remarked Martha.

"Me too," replied Gabriella. "I guess we should call it a night. Night everyone."

4

"Morning, hope you are all well rested and ready for our day?" said Susan. Once we have had breakfast we will meet outside and head off down to the River Thames for our boat trip."

Gabriella was feeling a bit tired still, but looking forward to the day.

Once they had reached the Thames they all boarded a boat, which was hired just for them, seeing that there were so many. It was a beautiful, sunny day and the river was nice and calm.

"Welcome aboard," announced the captain. "Our trip will take us down the river to Bankside, Blackfriars, Embankment and finally the London Eye. So sit back and enjoy some of the famous landmarks, I will tell you about some of them as we go along."

Gabriella was enjoying the smooth journey down the Thames, and the warm heat from the sun. This is so relaxing she smiled to herself.

"We are now coming up to the Tate Modern, known for its modern and contemporary art. Next is St Paul's Cathedral, where the funeral of Winston Churchill took place."

"Is that the man who smoked those big fat cigars?" laughed Martha.

"It certainly is," replied the captain. "He served as prime minister twice. 1940 to 1945, where he led Britain to victory in the Second World War, and then again in 1951 to 1955."

"Awesome," Petra burst out.

"In front of us is the Millennium Bridge, also known as the wobbly bridge due to some swaying motion on the first two days of it opening in 2000. It was closed for repairs and reopened in 2002."

"That must have been scary," replied Ingrid.

They were all having such a lovely time on the Thames, taking lots of photos and taking in the sights.

"We are now coming to our last famous landmark as our journey comes to an end" said the captain. The London Eye, also known as the Millennium Wheel. You can also see the most famous clock in London, Big Ben, and the Houses of Parliament, where Guy Fawkes attempted to blow it up in 1605."

"This is amazing," said Gabriella, "I'm loving London already!"

"Okay everyone," said Clare. "This is where we get off, can you please show your appreciation to the captain." Everyone gave the captain a round of applause. "Now we will be moving on to the London Eye."

Gabriella was very excited to be going on the London Eye, she had read so much about it and now she was actually going on it.

"As there are so many of us we have booked our own capsule to take us around. As we wait for our turn I will just briefly tell you about the London Eye. It was launched in the year 2000, it is one hundred and thirty-five metres high and takes thirty minutes to travel one revolution. It is one of the most popular attractions in London. Once inside you will find a three hundred and sixty-degree map which points out all the main points of interest across London.

Okay it is our turn to get on. Enjoy the ride and take in the beautiful sights of London."

"This is so exciting," echoed Ingrid as the door closed.

Slowly the wheel began to move. As they reached the top the views across London were amazing. Everyone was taking photos. Gabriella just stood there taking it all in and writing notes. After thirty minutes their journey had come to an end.

"Okay ladies and gents, we will now find a spot to sit and have lunch." They found a nice park where they could sit and relax in the sun.

Once lunch had finished they gathered their things together and headed towards the tube.

"Where are we going next?" asked Petra eagerly.

"Our next visit is to the Science Museum, stay close together please."

Inside the Science Museum they were greeted by their guide, Sean.

"Welcome to the Science Museum, I will be your guide for the next thirty minutes to tell you briefly about the museum, if there are any questions please ask. The museum was founded in 1857, it is world renowned for its historic collections, from the future to space travel. See, touch and experience the major scientific advances of the last three hundred years. There's lots for you to explore here at the museum, the best way to do that is to let you wander around yourselves, I hope you have an enjoyable visit."

"Right, we have the next five hours before the museum closes," Mark informed them. "There is a lot to see and do here, some things you will have to pay for, like the simulators and IMAX theatre, but there are also plenty of free exhibitions and galleries as well. We will meet up at the main entrance at six o'clock."

Where shall I start thought Gabriella, there is so much to see. Gabriella explored the history of veterinary medical treatment of animals in the past, instruments used for animal birth and slaughter which was not very pleasant but interesting.

Gabriella looked at the Agriculture gallery where they displayed the ploughs and hoes from the middle ages, to the combine harvesters and balers of the twentieth century, and even got to operate a cut-away combine harvester herself which was fun. Then she went and looked at glimpses of medical history where they showed medical dramas on board warships, and childbirth in Victorian times. Gabriella found that a little bit squeamish. Gabriella was having such a good time exploring so many things, before she knew it, it was nearly six o'clock. Better go and meet the others she thought.

Martha, Petra and Ingrid came bounding up to Gabriella.

"What did you think of that?" asked Ingrid.

"Amazing," replied Gabriella, "it was so fascinating, so much history in one place."

"I hope you all had a good time here at the museum?" enquired Mark. "We will head back to the hostel now where dinner should be ready for us, you must all be hungry by now? I know I am," he laughed.

Once they arrived back they all went and cleaned up before dinner. Everyone was so busy talking about their day.

"Okay ladies and gents, once you have all finished, the rest of the evening is yours, but taking a look at most of you I think it will be an early night!" They all laughed and nodded in agreement. "Tomorrow will be your day to do what you want, you all have our phone numbers in case you need to get in touch for any reason, and you also have your maps for the underground and buses. There will be an itinerary on the board in reception of what we will be doing in the coming days. So have a great day tomorrow."

Gabriella went back to her room and called her parents.

"Hi Mama"

"Bambino! Papa its Gabriella," mama put the phone onto speaker so they could both talk to her. "How are you?" they both asked. "What have you been doing, what is London like, have you made new friends, are you eating enough?"

"Slow down," laughed Gabriella. "I am having a wonderful time. London is an amazing place, and there is so much more to see yet. Yes, I have made new friends, and yes, I am eating enough! How is everything there?"

"Everything is good here," said mama. "The patisserie is very busy, Maria is helping us out until you come back. She misses you just as much as we do, your brothers are fine, working hard. It is quiet without you here bambino."

"The time will go fast mama. I have to go now, give my love to everyone and tell Maria I will be writing to her and the gang very soon. I love you mama, papa, speak to you soon."

Gabriella was feeling a little homesick after talking to her parents, but she was not going to let that get in the way of enjoying her time away. She lay on her bed thinking of where she would explore tomorrow as she slowly drifted off to sleep.

***

Gabriella woke up bright and early, as did her roommates.

"Morning everyone."

"Morning," they replied.

"So what are you all doing today?"

Martha and Ingrid decided to go Oxford Street shopping. Petra couldn't decide what to do.

"You can come with me if you like?" said Gabriella. "I am going to mass first at Westminster Cathedral then I was thinking of going to the Shard, I hear it is an amazing building."

"That would be nice. Thank you."

After breakfast, Gabriella and Petra headed off to the underground to get the tube to Westminster Cathedral.

"Wow this is a big church." Petra whispered as they entered.

"It sure is," Gabriella replied.

As they took their seats the choir started to sing, and the mass began.

After mass had finished Gabriella and Petra took a walk around the Cathedral

"This is so beautiful," remarked Gabriella. "The marble and the mosaics are just wonderful, and there are lots of lovely chapels."

They took lots of photos, as it was allowed now that mass had finished, and Gabriella wrote her notes, as she was keeping a journal of her adventures. What a lovely start to the day she thought.

After their visit to the cathedral they headed back to London Bridge to go see the famous Shard, London's highest viewing platform. As they entered the Shard they were guided to the lifts which took them to the very top, all ninety-five floors. There were shops, restaurants, bars, a hotel, you could even have private Yoga classes.

"Wow, this is incredible." Smiled Petra. "Look Gabriella, this view is spectacular!" They both just stood there taking it all in. You could see the entire city.

After spending an hour there visiting the shops and buying souvenirs, they went to a small café nearby for some lunch.

"Seeing that it is such a lovely day how about we go to Hyde Park and just chill out?" suggested Petra.

"Sounds like a good idea, let's make the most of the sunshine, you can never tell with the English weather how long it will last for!" They both laughed.

***

Their time in England was coming to an end. They had visited the Natural History Museum, Tower of London and Madam Tussauds. Their last place to see before they headed off to their next destination was Buckingham Palace.

"This will be our last London attraction to see before we head off tomorrow," explained Thomas. "Buckingham Palace, as you will all be aware of, is where the Queen of England sometimes resides. Once inside we will be guided around."

"Afternoon everyone. I am Malcolm your guide around the palace. Buckingham House, as it was first known, was bought by George III in 1761 for his wife, Queen Charlotte, where they had fifteen children, and one of their sons became King, King George the IV. In 1826, with the assistance of architect John Nash, he transformed the house into a palace. Many Kings and Queens have resided here over the years, up unto the present day with our Queen, Queen Elizabeth. Buckingham Palace is often the centre of state occasions and royal hospitality. The state rooms provide the setting for ceremonial occasions and official entertaining. There are many paintings and sculptures by Rubens, Rembrandt and Canova, also some of the finest English and French furniture in the world. There is a lovely garden café where you can purchase tea and coffee and enjoy the views across the famous lawns on this glorious, sunny day."

"That was very interesting," said Martha. "Fifteen children, how can anyone have fifteen children, and in those days!" They all laughed.

"It's time to head back to the hostel now," Clare informed everyone. "After we have had dinner you have some free time to do as you wish, but we have a very early start in the morning. Breakfast will be at six then we will be heading off to the airport."

5

All the bags had been checked in and everyone headed to the departure lounge. Gabriella was looking forward to Spain, she had never been before, saying that, she has never been outside of Italy!

"Flight V506 to Madrid is now boarding, can you please make your way to gate twenty-seven."

The flight to Madrid was lovely and smooth. Once landed, they all went to claim their bags.

"Welcome to Madrid" announced Susan. "Our coach should be outside waiting for us to take us to our accommodation, so if everyone is ready, let's go."

It was about an hour drive to the hostel which was near the centre of town. It was very hot. Thankfully the coach was air-conditioned.

"Okay, let's sort out the rooms, unpack and freshen up. There will be a traditional Spanish paella served for dinner this evening, plus something for those of you that don't eat shellfish. We will see you in the dining area at seven o'clock, so time for you to have a rest."

The four girls decided to share the same room again, as they got on so well with each other.

"It's so hot!" complained Ingrid.

"You will be fine, once we get changed out of our jeans and put some shorts on" advised Petra. "Well, first impressions so far?"

"Too hot!" laughed Ingrid, as they all threw their pillows at her.

"Too early to tell, ask me after dinner," replied Martha. "Speaking of, is it time yet? I'm starving!"

They all headed down to dinner, you could smell the lovely aromas down the hallway.

"I hope it tastes as good as it smells," added Martha.

"Welcome my friends, we are happy to have you here. My name is Samuel and I own this Establishment, with my wife, Mila and my two children, Juan and Camila. This evening we have prepared for you a traditional Spanish dish, paella, and for those who are not keen on shellfish we have Catalonia, which is grilled vegetables, served with rice, fried egg and tomato sauce. We hope you enjoy your meal. Please help yourselves."

Hmm looks lovely, what shall I have, thought Gabriella. Maybe a bit of each.

The room was buzzing with chat and the clatter of plates, plenty of wine and soft drinks.

"That was wonderful!" said Petra. They all nodded in agreement. "I'm so full, just what I needed. I know it's still early but if you all don't mind I 'm going to go lay down for a while."

"Actually, think we will join you," said the other girls.

Before they knew it they were all fast asleep.

"Morning all," boomed a bright and cheerful Martha. "Come on ladies, time to get up, it's a beautiful sunny day."

"How can you be so cheerful this time of the morning?" Said Petra as she looked at her watch. "Did we really sleep that long?"

"Knock, knock, breakfast in half an hour ladies, then we will be going to Prado Museum."

Once everyone was ready, they headed off to the museum. When they arrived they met with a tour guide who took them around and explained a bit about the art work.

"The museum houses one of the finest art collections. The best collection of Spanish paintings in the world by artists such as Goya, El Greco, Da Ribera and Velazquez. The most famous painting here in the museum is 'Las Meninas' by Velazquez, showing princess Margarita and her two ladies-in-waiting as well as the artist himself.

Goya's work makes up such a large part of the museum that his statue stands outside the main entrance. His painting of 'The Naked Maja' led him to being accused of obscenity.
I recommend the following pieces for you to look at, at your own leisure. 'The Crucifixion' by Juan de Flandes, 'Artemis' by Rembrandt, 'The Nobleman' with hand on his chest by El Greco and 'Jacob's Dream' by Jose da Ribera. Enjoy the rest of your visit."

"Gosh that was a lot to take in," said Ingrid, "think I need a cup of tea before we go and look at the rest!"

There was a cafeteria in the museum shop, where they could also buy any souvenirs.

"Did you know that Spain's greatest playwright Felix Lope de Vega y Carpio started writing when he was twelve years old and completed two thousand plays? Can you imagine that, two thousand? He was called the 'Shakespeare of Spanish literature,'" explained Petra.

"That's very interesting Petra but I really need some tea!"

"Ingrid!" They all laughed.

The tour of the museum was coming to an end.

"Okay folks," called Susan. "It is a beautiful day outside so we thought you might just like to chill out for a while. There is a lovely park not far away, you can go on a horse drawn carriage, go on a row boat or just sit and relax, and I think there may be some free concerts as well. Whatever you do just enjoy the rest of the afternoon, we will be heading back to the hostel around six thirty."

Gabriella wanted to just sit by herself for a while. A good time to write to the gang back home. As Gabriella was writing her letter, a beautiful butterfly came and rested on her shoulder.

"Do you know what butterflies stand for?" came this voice from nowhere.

Gabriella was quite startled.

"I'm sorry, I didn't mean to alarm you."

Gabriella gave a slight smile, feeling a bit uneasy.

"Butterflies mean freedom and spiritual transformation, to remind us that life's too short, so enjoy what time we have on the earth. They mean creativity, joy, change, new beginnings. Be like a butterfly, spread your wings and discover your true life's purpose."

And with that he just got up and left.

Gabriella sat there, not really sure of what just went on. As she looked around, the man was nowhere to be seen, but the butterfly was still there on her shoulder. She wondered what that was all about, and with that the butterfly just gently flew away. Gabriella continued writing her letter.

"Gabriella, come and join us," shouted Martha, we're going to go on a row boat around the lakes."

Gabriella laughed and went to join her friends.

It had been a really lovey relaxing day, the girls had such fun, but it was time to start heading back to the hostel.

After dinner Gabriella, Petra, Martha and Ingrid decided to go to a bar to see the flamenco dancers. It was quite busy with lots of tourists. They found a table to sit at and ordered a large jug of Sangria. They were really enjoying their evening.

"Let's get another jug of Sangria," laughed a tipsy Ingrid, as she got up to do her own version of a flamenco dance.

"I think all that sun has got to her head," joked Petra.

"You mean the Sangria," laughed Gabriella.

It was getting on for midnight and time to go back to the hostel. They didn't have such an early start the next morning so they could have a bit of a lay in.

Ten thirty the following morning there was a knock at the door.

"Time to get up ladies, we will be heading out around midday," informed Thomas.

Ingrid just pulled the covers back over her very sore head. "I don't think I can manage it today."

The other girls just laughed.

"What's wrong Ingrid, too much Sangria last night?" mocked Petra.

"Leave me alone, I think I'm going to be sick" she said as she rushed to the bathroom.

"You better stay here today," Martha advised, "and sleep it off."

Today they were going to the cable cars. They took the short journey by bus.

"Okay," Thomas announced. "Each car holds five people, it only takes eleven minutes, a short journey but it has great views. There is a small leaflet that tells you about what you can see. We stop off at Casa de Campo Park, where I will tell you what happens there."

Gabriella, Petra, Martha and two others went in one car. As the car started to ascend, they could see the Western park, the train station Principe Pio, the chapel of San Antonio de la Florida and the Manzanares River.

"These views are beautiful," gasped Petra. "Did you know that the total length of the cable is four thousand, eight hundred feet, and that it travels eleven feet per second?"

"Thank you for that piece of information tour guide Petra." They all laughed.

They had now reached the Casa de Campo Park, which is Madrid's largest park. It was formally a royal hunting estate and where Madrid families usually head to on sunny days. There was plenty to do for everyone. There were pony rides, a maze, carousel, a rollercoaster, indoor paintball, and for the sportier type, mountain bikes, football, tennis, swimming and much more. It also had its own zoo that had around three thousand animals from all countries, as well as a large aquarium and a dolphin tank.

"There is plenty to do here," remarked Mark. "You have the rest of the day to enjoy this lovely park, we will meet back here at the cable cars at five thirty."

"So much to choose from," commented Martha. "How about we go in the maze and see how long it takes us to get out?"

The girls had such a laugh going around the maze, taking all the wrong turnings. Finally, after forty five minutes they found their way out.

"That was so much fun" laughed Gabriella. "I thought we would never get out. Let's go on a pony now, I have never been on one before."

"Don't you think we are a bit old for pony rides, Gabriella?"

"Oh Petra, you are only as old as you feel, and at the moment I feel like a child again," chuckled Gabriella.

So off they went, on a pony ride.

"My bottom is so sore," muttered Petra. "How on earth do people ride horses for hours? I have been on a pony for five minutes and can hardly walk!"

Gabriella and Martha couldn't stop laughing.

Next stop was the aquarium and dolphin tank. There were so many beautiful fish, all different shapes, colours and sizes, but Gabriella was drawn to the dolphin tank.

What beautiful creatures she thought, she just stood there gazing at them, it was like she was in a trance. There was one particular dolphin that had a black patch on his tail that kept swimming by. As he swam by again he stopped and pressed his nose up to the glass of the tank, and Gabriella moved closer. They just looked at each other, it was as if they had met before. Gabriella couldn't take her eyes of this beautiful creature, it was strange, like the dolphin was trying to communicate with her. Gabriella could feel herself being drawn in more, it was like she was in the tank with the dolphin. She felt so peaceful as if it was just the two of them there.

"Gabriella, Gabriella, come and see this!"

Gabriella came out of her trance, she seemed a bit dazed. The dolphin swam off and continued circling the tank.

"Are you okay?" asked Petra. "You look a bit strange."

"Yes, I'm fine," she replied as she went over to see the fish.

What on earth was that all about! Gabriella felt very peaceful but a bit spaced out like she wasn't really there. Maybe I need something to eat.

After they had eaten, they continued around the park having fun until it was time to leave.

Once they had got back to the hostel, Gabriella went and laid on her bed, still trying to figure out what had gone on with the dolphin.

"Did you all miss me?" bellowed Ingrid.

"Well you seem a lot better," observed Martha.

"I feel fine thank you. It's amazing what a good sleep and a few bottles of water can do. Just don't let me get like that again," she smiled.

After they had all gone for dinner they went back to their room and spent the rest of the evening chatting.

The next day was their last day in Madrid, they were going on an opened topped bus tour. The bus pickup point was a five-minute walk from the hostel. As they all gathered waiting for the bus, Gabriella's mind started to wander. First the strange encounter with the guy and the butterfly, then the bazar thing that happened with the dolphin, she was trying to figure it all out but was coming up with nothing. The bus arrived and they went on board.

"Bienvenida, welcome" said the bus driver. "On our tour you will find a map on each seat showing you some of the main attractions. If you sit on the upper deck you will be able to enjoy the marvellous views of Madrid's monuments and sights. There are headphones so you can listen to ongoing commentary supplying information about the sights which is in eight different languages. Our journey will last approximately seventy-five minutes and you are welcome to hop on and off the bus and explore at any time. You can hop on another bus to continue your journey, or to take you back to your destination. So sit back and enjoy the ride."

There were lots of interesting things to see from the top of the bus. They passed Museo Del Prado art museum, Puerta de Alcaia neo-classical monument, Templo de Debod an ancient Egyptian temple, Teatro Real opera house, Gran Via known as the Spanish Broadway, the street that never sleeps because of its nightlife. There was one particular place they were approaching, Cathedral Almudena, a catholic cathedral that caught Gabriella's attention.

"I'm getting off here girls, I'll see you back at the hostel."

The cathedral was beautiful. It is the most important religious building in Madrid, the first cathedral to be consecrated outside of Rome. Gabriella went and knelt down in one of the pews. She prayed for her family and friends back in Italy, and the new friends she had made on her journey. She also prayed about the strange things that had happened whilst being in Madrid with the butterfly and dolphin, as she could not make any sense of it all.

After half an hour of prayer, Gabriella got up and walked around the cathedral taking in the peace and quietness, admiring its beauty before she left. Gabriella hopped back on a bus that took her back to the hostel and waited for the others to return.

"Where did you go?" asked Petra.

"Oh I just wanted to go to the cathedral, my mother will want to know that I've been going to church!" she laughed. "Well this is our last night in Madrid, what shall we do?"

"Let's just wander round the city and see where it leads us, as long as there is no drink involved," proclaimed Ingrid.

The girls had a lovely evening wandering around the city, checking out the shops and just observing the Spanish culture, but it was time to head back to the hostel to pack, ready for an early start to the airport for their next destination.

6

They were on their way now to the beautiful Portuguese island of Madeira. They flew into the capital, Funchal.

"Wow did you see that runway? I thought we were going to go over the edge it was so short," said a nervous Ingrid.

"It used to be a lot smaller," explained one of the air stewards. "It was one of the world's most dangerous airport runways until it was extended in the year 2000. But don't worry, it's very safe now."

"Glad to hear it," grimaced Ingrid.

It was a lovely warm day, not too hot. The coach ride from the airport was about twenty-five minutes. All you could see were mountains one side and ocean on the other, it was very beautiful. Once they reached the hostel they unpacked their bags and had lunch.

"Guys if you want to have a look around, there are some leaflets at reception," announced Clare. "If you do, try not to go too far today until you get use to your surroundings, or you can stay here at the hostel if you want to just relax. I will be putting a note of our agenda under your door after we have had our evening meal."

The girls decided to stay at the hostel. Gabriella called home, as did Martha. The evening quickly went by. They now had their timetable for the coming weeks, starting with a seven o'clock wake up call, breakfast, then off to visit the Monte Palace Tropical Gardens and the Madeira embroidery museum.

The coach picked them up the following morning to take them to the gardens. On their arrival they were given a guide map and an information sheet.

"Did you know, The Monte Palace was donated by entrepreneur, Jose Berardo in 1988 where he created his dream, a tropical garden that he could share with the world." Informed Petra. "There are also exotic plants and trees both native and from around the world, including Azaleas and orchids from the Himalayas, and Heather from Scotland."

"Here she goes again!" mocked Ingrid, rolling her eyes.

"What! I'm just sharing a bit of information with you."

"Petra, that's why they give us information sheets, so we can just read about these things," laughed Gabriella and Martha.

"There is also a museum."

"PETRA!"

"Okay, I'll be quiet."

As they were wandering around the gardens they came to a lake where there were some beautiful white swans, ducks and gorgeous peacocks strutting around, showing off their colourful plumage. Then they discovered the oriental gardens with their many Asian sculptures, stone benches with oriental decorations and various stone lanterns. There was also a lake of Koi fish. It was one of the most interesting and beautiful gardens in Madeira.

After a few hours, the group moved on to their next attraction.

The Madeira Embroidery Museum was quite small, but it housed the most beautiful embroidery, tapestry and handiwork, especially wickerwork. The centrepiece of the museum was the collection of valuable ninetieth and early twentieth century embroidered cloths and decorative pieces. Embroidery is one of Madeira's historic crafts. You will usually find Madeiran ladies by the harbour making embroidered napkins.

"Look at all of these beautiful cloths," described Gabriella. "My mother would love some of these, the detail in them are just stunning. I think I will buy her some."

It didn't take long to look around the museum. They made their purchases then headed out for lunch.

As there were twenty of them, they split into two groups to go and have lunch. They found two cafes close to each other and sat outside enjoying the warmth of the sun and listening to the local music.

Once lunch was over, the two groups came back together.

"We have had a busy morning," began Mark, "so now it's free time, so go and explore and we will meet up at six o'clock. Our meeting point will be outside the church on the corner of this road. If there are any problems give one of us a call."

The girls stuck together as usual. They looked in art and craft shops, and souvenir shops where they bought post cards to send home to family and friends. Then they came across a small shop that made glass bead accessories. It was a family run business that sold the most beautiful necklaces, bracelets and even salad servers! You could stand and watch the lady actually make them in front of you.

"These are beautiful, look at this bracelet, the detail that has gone into it, I'm going to buy this for my sister, and that necklace for my mum, and the keychain for my grandmother!" Martha was like a child in a candy store.

Gabriella found the perfect gift for Maria, a bracelet with all of Marias favourite colours.

As they walked along the cobbled street of Municipal Square they found a book shop called Fundacao Livraria Esperance. When they opened the door to go in they could not believe their eyes, it was like being transported into book heaven.

"Wow. I have never seen so many books in one place before," remarked Ingrid. "It's amazing."

There were three floors of wall to wall books. Books for every age, every genre, every interest and in many different languages. There were rare editions, first editions. Nothing could prepare you for the amount of time spent there. Even if you weren't a real book lover, you soon became one!

By the time the girls dragged themselves away, it was time to meet the others outside the church.

"I hope you all had a good time exploring and found lots to see? We will be going back to the hostel now for dinner, then the evening is yours."

Back at the hostel and after dinner the girls showed each other what they had bought. They bought pretty much the same. Glass bead bracelets, necklaces, key rings, embroidered cloths and napkins, and of course some books. Then they wrote out their postcards.

"Let's see what we have tomorrow," yawned a tired Martha. "A leisurely four hour Levada walk. Best get some sleep then, I can feel those sore muscles already! Night everyone."

"Night," they all replied.

Nine thirty and the coach arrived to take them to Queimadas Caldeirao Verde for their Levada walk where they were met by their guides, Manuel and Pedro.

"Good morning ladies and gentleman. Welcome to Queimadas Caldeirao Verde. I hope you have plenty of water to drink and comfortable shoes on, it is a fairly moderate footpath but there are some rough pathways along the way. We have sticks to help you on the hike and torches for when we go through the tunnels. I ask you please to stick to the pathways. On our walk you will see excellent specimens of elegant Japanese cedars, Lilly of the valley trees, Madeira blueberry, which will be seen along the trail plus different kinds of birds and waterfalls.

This Levada walk was built in the eighteenth century, nowadays it is part of our rich heritage left by our ancestors. It has a high altitude of nine hundred metres above sea level so if any of you feel a bit light headed, just rest when you need to, it will pass as you get used to it. I will be leading at the front and Pedro will be at the back if you need assistance. Ladies, there are no toilets on the walk so if you need to go I suggest you use the toilets that are here before we start."

"Light headed, high altitude, hike, I thought we were going on a nice leisurely walk!" groaned Ingrid.

The other girls laughed.

"Okay. If everyone is ready, we will start our walk."

They were about half way up when they started to feel the difference in altitude, but everyone coped very well with it, even Ingrid! They were surrounded by the most luxurious dense ever green laurel forests. Further up they went through the amazing hand carved tunnels, even though it wasn't too dark they still needed to put their torch on for that added light. When they came out of each tunnel they were greeted by the most beautiful waterfalls.

The spectacular cliff edges, with their breath taking views, overlooked the landscapes and the village of Sao Jorge. They rested here for a while taking photos and absorbing the pure beauty of it all.

They finally reached the end of the hike, arriving at Caldeirao Verde Lake with its one-hundred-metre-high, breath taking waterfall, falling on the cold and crystalline lagoon.

"We will rest here now for about an hour and have lunch, you are free to have a wander round but please do not go too far."

"Thank goodness for that, I don't think I could have walked another inch," groaned Ingrid, collapsing to the ground.

After lunch Gabriella took herself off to admire the beautiful surroundings. She went and sat on a rock close to the waterfall. Gabriella got her note pad out and started writing. This is one of the most beautiful tranquil places I have ever seen. She closed her eyes for a moment soaking up the peace and quiet with just the sounds of water washing through her mind. She felt something on her hand, as she looked down there was a butterfly.

"Hello beautiful," she found herself saying, "where have you come from?"

Her thoughts immediately went back to Spain where the butterfly landed on her shoulder, and the disappearing man that spoke to her about the meaning of butterflies. This was all quite strange. With that the butterfly flew away and Gabriella continued with her writing trying not to think about it.

"Okay everyone it's time to start making our way back down," announced Manuel.

Even though the views were very beautiful some of them were glad it was over! At least the walk down was less tiring.

Once they reached the bottom they handed back the sticks and torches to Manuel and Pedro, and thanked them for their day. They boarded the coach and made their way back to the hostel.

By the time they arrived back they were all exhausted.

"Listen up everyone," said Thomas. I know you must all be very tired, it has been a long day and I'm sure there will

be a few sore feet and aching legs tomorrow! So for the
next few days it will be time for you to just relax and do as
you wish. Dinner will be ready in half hour for those of
you who want to freshen up."

"Think I am going to stay in bed for the next few days I
can just about move," muttered Ingrid. Petra agreed.

They all slept really well that night not waking until
eleven o'clock the next morning.

"Is that the time? Ahh every bone in my body aches,"
groaned Ingrid as she tried to get out of bed. "I don't think
I'll be doing much today. Does anyone else feel like this or
is it just me?"

"I actually feel okay," replied Gabriella.

Martha and Petra just lay there moaning.

"I don't know what your plans are girls but I am going to
go and find a nice place to have some breakfast, well I
should say brunch and enjoy the Madeiran sunshine. I'll
see you later, have a nice rest."

Gabriella found a lovely little patisserie. She ordered some
coffee and a selection of pastries and sat outside just
watching the people go by. It reminded her a bit of home.
She got her note pad out and wrote about yesterday's
walk. When Gabriella had finished she took a stroll down
to the harbour where the cruise ships had parked up. Pirate
boats and catamarans sailed by on the beautiful blue
ocean.

"What a lovely sight," came this voice beside Gabriella.

Gabriella turned to see who it was.

"Excuse me, I didn't mean to interrupt you. The ocean is such a magical place; it just draws you in."

Gabriella didn't say anything, she just nodded her head in agreement and smiled.

"Are you here on vacation?" he asked.

"Yes. I'm traveling around Europe with a group of other people."

"And what do you think of this beautiful island?"

"I've not seen too much of it, but what I have seen I like," replied Gabriella.

"I hope you don't think I'm being too forward but would you like to have a coffee? There is a café just down here."

Gabriella wasn't sure. She knew nothing about this man but for some reason it was like she had known him for a long time.

"That would be nice, thank you."

As they ordered coffee they introduced themselves.

"My name is Macario."

"Are you Italian?" enquired Gabriella. "It sounds like an Italian name."

"Yes, well Italian and Portuguese. My mother is Italian and my Father is Portuguese so they found a name that suited both nationalities."

"I'm Gabriella, I am also Italian."

"Where in Italy are you from?"

"A town called Positano."

"You are kidding me. My mother is from Praiano, it's not far from Positano. I've been there several times. What a small world!"

"So do you live in Madeira or Italy?"

"Mostly in Madeira. I go to Italy for work some times and when I want to get away for a while. Have you always lived in Positano?"

"Yes, ever since I was born, my parents have lived there all their lives. They have their own patisserie. What do you do?"

"I work for my father, he owns a chain of restaurants both here and in Italy and he wants to expand into other countries. I do a variety of jobs, from hiring staff to looking out for new premises."

Gabriella could not believe what she was hearing. First that his mother is from Italy and not far from where she comes from, both families have businesses in the food industry and that her brother Michael wants to own his own restaurant just as Macario's family do. She just sat there with a slight grin on her face.

"Have I said something amusing?" asked Macario.

"No. It's just one of my brothers has just qualified as a chef in Paris hoping to own is own restaurant one day."

They both looked at each other and laughed. They talked for hours, they had so much in common. It was quite spooky!

"I didn't realise we had been here so long. I guess I should be going," added Gabriella.

"Do you have to? I can show you some of the most beautiful sights on the island and maybe dinner?"

Gabriella wasn't sure, she had only just meet Macario but it seemed like she had always known him. It didn't take her long to decide.

"That sounds very nice, but I really must go back to the hostel so that the others know I'm okay and so I can change."

"Great, give me the address of the hostel and I'll pick you up later, say six o'clock?"

"Looking forward to it."

Gabriella walked in to the hostel with a big grin on her face.

"What are you smiling about?" asked Petra. And where have you been, we were wondering where you were?"

"Sorry if I worried you, I have had a lovely afternoon in the company of a very nice young man, and now I am going to get ready as he is picking me up for dinner."

"WHAT!" screeched Ingrid "What do you know about this man? He could be a criminal, or worse."

Gabriella laughed.

"Ingrid its fine. I just have a really good feeling about him, you would not believe how much we have in common and his mother is from a town not far from me in Italy."

"He could just be saying that to trick you! Do you want us to follow you so you feel safer?"

"I will be fine, I promise, but thank you for caring."

Macario picked Gabriella up as he said at six o'clock.

"You look lovely."

"Thank you."
Macario took Gabriella to a small family run bar where they sat outside in the warm evening sun, then they went for dinner in a quiet Portuguese restaurant where they drank wine and just talked and talked.

"It's strange but it feels like I have always known you Gabriella."

"I know; I feel the same. Is it really possible to feel so connected after just one day?"

"I don't know," replied Macario, "it's never happened before, I can't explain it but it just feels right."

They talked about everything and anything, they were enjoying each other's company so much they didn't realise what time it was.

"I really think I should be going now. I didn't know it was so late. I have had a really lovely evening. Thank you."

Macario walked Gabriella back to the hostel.

"Can I see you tomorrow? he asked.

"I would like that."

"Well good night then."

"Night."

The girls were waiting up for Gabriella just to make sure she got back safely.

"Did you have a good evening?" asked Martha.

"I had a wonderful evening thank you."

They sat up for ages as Gabriella told them about Macario and their evening.

7

The next morning all the girls were up early. Petra, Martha and Ingrid felt a lot better after their day of rest. They all went down for breakfast together.

"So Gabriella, where is Macario taking you?"

"I have no idea. I guess a look around the Island. It's certainly a lovely day for it."

After a filling breakfast of pancakes, a cheese and mushroom omelette and coffee, Gabriella went and got ready for Macario's arrival.

Macario took Gabriella to the town centre, they looked around the shops, went to the coffee bars, sat and listened to people singing in the streets and just enjoyed being in each other's company.

"There's something I want to show you, but we need to take the cable car."

They took the cable car up to the mountains, where there was the Igreja De Nossa Senhora do Monte - Our Lady of the Mount Church. They had to climb about fifty odd steep steps to get to the church but it was worth it.

"This looks beautiful," said Gabriella.

"Wait till you get inside, it's even more beautiful," Macario told her.

When they entered the church Gabriella was taken away by the beauty of the interior. It was so tranquil and peaceful. Macario told Gabriella a bit about the church.

"It was built in the eighteenth century to commemorate the appearance of the Virgin Mary to a shepherd girl in the 1400s, it also houses the tomb of Charles I of Austria, the last of the Hapsburg Emperors exiled to Madeira following World War 1 where he died in 1922."

"Well you certainly know your history," laughed Gabriella.

"My mother used to bring me here quite a lot as a child, she found this church to be the most peaceful and away from the streets."

"I can understand why," replied Gabriella.

They went up to the bell tower which over looked Funchal, the views were stunning, you could see across the Atlantic.

"This is beautiful Macario."

"Just as beautiful as you, Gabriella."

Gabriella felt her face redden, and her tummy felt like butterflies fluttering around.

"Can we go and sit in the pews for a bit?" asked Gabriella. "I want to take this memory away with me."

They sat for about half an hour in silence. Gabriella prayed and thanked God for this beautiful day and for bringing her and Macario together, even if it was for only a short time.

As they came out of the church Macario asked Gabriella if she wanted him to take her photo.

"Only if you are in it with me," said a slightly shy Gabriella.

So they asked a passer-by to take their photo. Then they took the toboggan ride back down to the bottom.

"How about we grab some lunch, then I want to take you on the catamaran."

"Sounds perfect," Gabriella replied.

The ocean was still and calm, the ideal day for going on the catamaran to enjoy the tranquillity of the Madeiran coastline.

Macario and Gabriella sat at the front of the catamaran on the netting.

"We might get a bit wet here from the sprays of the water, are you okay with that?"

"That's fine," smiled Gabriella.

It was so beautiful out on the ocean, the blue skies, the warmth of the sun, the peace. It felt magical. As they got further out to sea they saw some sea turtles and whales.

Gabriella got her camera out and started to video these beautiful creatures of the sea. Then out of nowhere, a dolphin swam close to the catamaran. It poked its head out of the water. Nobody could believe what they were seeing. Everyone was trying to get as close to the side as they could to take photos. The dolphin just seemed to be focusing on Gabriella, then it started to make noises as if it was trying to communicating with her. Gabriella moved a bit further to the front of the catamaran, as she did the dolphin followed her. She moved further round and still the dolphin continued to follow her.

"You are blessed." Macario smiled at Gabriella. "Dolphins are very spiritual creatures."

Gabriella sat back in her original place, followed by the dolphin. Gabriella reached out her hand, the dolphin came up to the surface and gently pushed her hand with its nose, then it disappeared.

One of the attendants came over to Gabriella.

"In all the years I have been working on these catamarans, I have never seen a dolphin come this close before. I know they like to follow boats but to actually see someone get that close to touch a dolphin is something I have never seen. You seem to have a special connection with them."

Gabriella smiled and looked at Macario, not really knowing what to say, but it did make her think about her last encounter with a dolphin at the aquarium in Spain. Was there something to this? They continued enjoying the beautiful views of the Atlantic.

As their journey came to an end, one of the other passengers came up to Gabriella.

"Young lady there is something very spiritual about you, I felt it throughout the whole trip. Not just your connection with the dolphin, but you have a beautiful aura too. I feel you will be doing something special, maybe here on the Island."

Gabriella felt a bit overwhelmed. She didn't know what was happening.

Over dinner Gabriella told Macario about her experiences with the butterflies and dolphins in Spain, and how she didn't understand what any of it meant.

"You know butterflies and dolphins are very spiritual," explained Macario. "Butterflies represent joy, freedom, creativity, change and new beginnings. Dolphins represent peace and harmony, compassion, caring, joy, playfulness and inner strength. They remind us to look for the good in everyone, to strive and bring peace to our lives and those around us."

"How do you know so much about these things?" asked Gabriella.

"Besides my parents being Catholic, they are also very spiritual people and know that animals can be too. They believe that there are no such things as coincidences, that when things happen they happen for a reason. When you are blessed with a gift, use that gift. I guess it's something I've just grown up with. The ocean is one of the most inspiring places to be around, it helps you look at your inner self, it's a good place to think."

"Macario, you know I have to leave in two days to continue my travels. This is going to sound crazy but why do I feel so drawn to you?"

"It doesn't sound crazy Gabriella, when things are meant to be they are meant to be, so my mother would say! You were brought to this Island for a reason. Let us enjoy the rest of our day together and let fate lead the way!"

Their day was coming to an end. Macario took Gabriella back to the hostel.

"I guess this is it then."

"Gabriella you make it sound like it's the end, trust me, it's just the beginning. Where else are you going in Europe?"

"Next stop is Greece then Malta, Germany, France then back home to Italy."

"I have to go to Paris in the next few months to look at some premises. My father wants to start up a restaurant or two there. I'm not sure of the dates yet but if I can make it so it falls in the same time you're there, we can see each other then. What do you think?"

"I think that sounds wonderful!" Gabriella threw her arms around Macario.

"I'm sorry I shouldn't have done that." She drew herself away.

Macario gently pulled Gabriella back towards him and kissed her.

"I think those butterflies have come back, but in my tummy this time!" laughed Gabriella.

"I feel it too. We have one another's phone number, we can text each other even if it's to just say hello and nothing else."

As Macario turned to walk away he looked back at Gabriella.

"Remember we have a date in Paris!"

"Welcome back stranger, we thought you had abandoned us!" joked Petra as Gabriella walked in. "So how was your day?"

Gabriella told them everything that happened, which took up the rest of the evening.

"How romantic! I wish I could meet someone that swept me off my feet like that." Gushed Ingrid.

"You never know what's around the corner Ingrid," smiled Gabriella.

The last two days were gone in a flash and then they were on their way to Athens Greece.

8

"Gabriella, Gabriella! Are you with us?" asked Martha.

"Sorry, I was miles away. What's up?"

"We're here, remember Greece, Athens. Come on daydreamer or you will be left on the plane!"

Gabriella's mind was elsewhere; she couldn't stop thinking about Macario. Why do I have such strong feelings for someone I hardly know?

When they arrived at the hostel they were greeted by their host and hostess Grigori and Eppie.

"Welcome to your home for the next two weeks, we hope you will be comfortable here. We provide breakfast only which is served from 6.30am till 9am. If you have any questions, one of us is normally around. Enjoy your stay here in Athens."

"Okay guys, once we have settled into our rooms we will meet at reception and go and find somewhere to have dinner," announced Clare.

The rooms were pretty basic, as were all of the hostels. Beds, two wardrobes, two sets of drawers which they had to share and a communal bathroom, but they were always clean. After an hour they all met for dinner. They found a nice Greek restaurant that was large enough to host all of them.

Once they were all seated and given menus, their waiter came and took their orders. Now as you can imagine this took a little while to get around them all. They started off with a Meze - a selection of toasted pitta chips, hummus, tzatziki, dolmades (stuffed vine leaves), keftedakia arni (crisp lamb meatballs), different cheeses, and a glass or two of Ouzo before their main course.

"What a lovely friendly restaurant," added Martha, "very authentic."

They were having a lovely evening enjoying the food, wine, music and friendly service but time was getting on and they had an early start the following day. They headed back to the hostel for a good night's sleep.

Everyone was up bright and early ready for breakfast. There was a lovely selection of cereals, Greek yoghurt with honey and walnuts, olive bread, omelette, spinach pie, and cold cuts of meat, grilled smokey sausage, olives, sesame bars, different cheeses and pastries. Plenty to fill them up, all set for their day.

Their first excursion was to the Acropolis. Accompanied by a tour guide, they were taken on a trek up on a high rocky outcrop above the city of Athens, which did not amuse Ingrid!

"Welcome to Athens historical monument the Acropolis, where the remains of several ancient buildings of great architectural and historic significance stand. The term Acropolis means upper city. Many of the city states of ancient Greece are built around an Acropolis, where the inhabitants could go as a place of refuge in times of invasion. It is for this reason that the most sacred buildings are usually on the Acropolis. As little as one hundred and fifty years ago there were still dwellings on the Acropolis. The most famous building is the Parthenon or the Temple of Athena."

"So what happened to the buildings? I understand that they were re constructed," enquired Martha
"That's correct," replied the guide, "the temple was built between 447 and 438BC. The Acropolis had been the site of an older temple and other monuments which had been destroyed by the Persians, where the people of Athens evacuated the city. When the Persians were defeated, columns from the older buildings were used in the construction of the Acropolis walls as a reminder of what Athens had suffered."

"You say that Parthenon is also called the Temple of Athena, who was Athena?" asked Martha again.

"Athena was the Greek goddess of wisdom and war, who the people considered their patron. The Athenians were very grateful to her for helping them win the war against Persia. They built a forty-foot statue of Athena and dedicated the temple to her."

"What a fascinating story," said Petra.

After the tour had finished they all took photos, there were even some artists amongst the group who would sketch everywhere they visited. Then they made their way back down to the bottom.

"Okay guys!" Mark raised his voice to be heard. "We will take a couple of hours to sit and have lunch and have a bit of a look around, there are quite a few taverns and cafes. We will meet back here then head off to the Acropolis Museum."

The girls found a lovely tavern to have their lunch. It was such a lovely day so they sat outside. Gabriella ordered a lovely lemon and garlic chicken with spinach and some crusty bread. Petra went for Moussaka. Ingrid had Pasta salad with feta cheese and Martha ordered chicken and salad in a pitta bread. They all had sparkling water.

As they were waiting for their food to arrive, Gabriella received a text message from Macario. She felt those butterflies in her tummy again. What's wrong with you, its only a text message she thought. As she started to read it her face began to redden slightly.

'Thought I would say hello and to know that you arrived safely in Athens? Things here are quite busy with the restaurants. I miss your lovely smile. Text back when you can. Macario x'

"Are you ok?" asked Martha. "Your face has gone red."

"Yes I'm fine thank you."

Gabriella replied. *'Arrived safely thank you. We went to see the Acropolis which was very interesting, having lunch now then off to the Acropolis Museum. I hope you are well. Speak soon. Gabriella x'*

Gabriella felt like a silly school girl not knowing what to say.

Their food arrived, they enjoyed every bit of it before returning to meet the others for their next trip.

When they reached the museum they were assigned another tour guide who explained some of the history of the museum.

"The Acropolis Museum is housed in this modern building set at the foot of the Acropolis. Many of the sculptures and relics that were found on the Acropolis are displayed here. The first museum opened in 1878, but the building was too small to accommodate both sculptures and vast amount of visitors so a new museum was built. It was designed by Swiss architect Bernard Tschumi and opened in 2009, the museum consists of sculptures that were found on the Acropolis hill. As you can see there is a glass floor where you will see the excavated remains of houses that have been uncovered? Also as you may have noticed, the surrounding of the building is all glass. That's so you can get a clear view to the Acropolis. Let us move to the next floor.

The gallery on this floor shows a large number of archaic statues from the fifth and sixth century BC. The museums most famous archaic sculpture is the Moschophoros, sculptured in 570BC representing a man named Rombos, who plans to sacrifice a calf. Further on you will see the statue of a boy named Kritios, which symbolizes the transition from archaic art to classical art. Then there is the beautiful relief of the young goddess Athena."

"As you can see there are a vast amount of statues and relics in the museum. I will briefly explain some of them to you then you can carry on at your own leisure."

"Next floor. Sculptures and reliefs from the Parthenon, the building you saw at the Acropolis. The majority of the original Parthenon sculptures, now known as the Elgin Marbles, are in the British Museum in London England.

Two thirds were obtained by the British ambassador to the Ottoman court Lord Elgin, which were then purchased from the British parliament and presented to the British Museum in 1816."

"What's an Elgin Marble?" asked Ingrid.

"They are marble statues from the Parthenon," replied Petra.

"So why don't they call them the Parthenon Marbles?"

"They are known as the Parthenon Marbles, but because Lord Elgin obtained and took them to England, they became the Elgin Marbles."

"Well that's not a very nice thing to do, claiming to be your marble statues when they belong to someone else!"

"No Ingrid it's not!" laughed Petra.

"Next floor. This is where I will leave you to carry on with your tour. There is a restaurant and retail if you wish to purchase anything. If you go out on to the terrace you will have a magnificent view of the Acropolis. Thank you for your time and enjoy the rest of your day."

"What an interesting tour," exclaimed Martha, "a lot of information to absorb?"

"Talking of information," replied Petra, "did you know that they use special glass around the building to protect the sculptures and visitors from excessive heat?"

The girls just looked at each other and burst out laughing.

"Why are you laughing? It's true!" asked a puzzled Petra.

"Oh Petra why have a tour guide when we have you!"

After a very long day it was time to head back to the hostel.

"Are you ok Gabriella?" asked Martha. "You seem to be very quiet today, like you're somewhere else."

"I'm fine, just thinking of home. I think I'll give my parents a call."

Gabriella called her parents and had a long chat with them, letting them know about her day, but she really needed to talk about what was going on in her head with Macario and her parents were not the right people to discuss this with, so she called Maria.

"Gabby, oh my word I can't believe I'm talking to you. How are you, are you having fun and what's wrong!?"

"Nothing's wrong, can't I call my best friend for a chat?"

"Gabby, it's me you're talking to, I know you better than anyone, what's wrong?"

Gabriella told Maria all about Macario and how she was feeling.

"I don't know what to do Maria. Why do I have these strong feelings for someone I hardly know? There's a really strong connection between us, it's like we have known each other forever."

"Gabby slow down. Sometimes things happen that we can't explain, if it's meant to be then it's meant to be! Concentrate on your travels, you know the ones that you've dreamt about all your life! Enjoy it, have fun, and see what happens when you see him in France."

"Thanks Maria, I knew I could count on you for words of wisdom! I better go this call is costing me a fortune." They both laughed. "Love you, speak soon."

"Well you look happier," observed Martha, "I guess the chat with your parents helped?"

"You could say that," smiled Gabriella.

9

The following morning a coach collected everyone from the hostel for a trip to the Kaisariani Monastery, a divinely meditative place surrounded by the serene forest park. Today was for them all to just take in the beautiful scenery and enjoy the tranquillity of this spiritual sanctuary.

"We will be here for the morning, before heading back to the hostel where I have arranged a small buffet to celebrate a special birthday of one of our party," explained Clare. "I know she won't mind me telling you, but its Joan's fiftieth birthday today. Happy birthday Joan!" Everyone gave her a round of applause. "We will meet back here at the coach at around one o'clock."

"This is lovely, so quiet, looks like we're the only ones here," whispered Martha.

"Why are you whispering Martha if we're the only ones here?" Ingrid bellowed.

"Ingrid keep it down, it is a spiritual place of tranquillity and calm, you're supposed to take in the beauty of the surroundings," replied Martha.

"There is a serene forest park with shady trees, cypresses, Mediterranean shrubs and vibrant flowers just up here," added Petra.

"How on earth do you do it, Petra? We've only been here five minutes and you know about the place already!" teased Ingrid.

"It's called picking up the leaflet at the gate that you lot obviously didn't see!"

They all laughed.

"Well seeing as you're the one with all the information, you can be our tour guide," Ingrid decided.

As they worked their way around the grounds, Petra told them about the Monastery.

"The monastery was named after a spring that once channelled water to a sanctuary of Aphrodite. From this spring the Emperor Hadrian funnelled the water to an aqueduct supplying fresh water. The pure crystal waters of Kaisariani spring were, and still continue to be credited with healing powers, particularly for women who wish to bear children."

"So you're telling me that if you were to drink water from the spring you would get pregnant?" asked Ingrid.

"I guess so?" replied Petra. "It seems that Aphrodite blessed the stream so that Greek brides would conceive quicker."

"So remind me who Aphrodite is?" enquired Ingrid.

"Aphrodite is the Greek goddess of love, desire and beauty, she was also the mother of the Greek god of love, Eros.

"I knew that," said an embarrassed Ingrid.

"Apparently the monastery was built over the ruins of a Roman Temple in the eleventh century. Four columns of the ancient temple survived and support the dome of the monastery's church. They say that the monastery has stood on holy ground since antiquity. In 1981, an earthquake did a lot of damage to the Byzantine bath house which has not yet been restored, so entrance is forbidden."

"For a small place there's a lot of history to it," remarked Martha. "Why don't we go and check out this forest?"

"You guys carry on, I want to have a wander round," said Gabriella. "Remember to be back by one o'clock."

What a peaceful place Gabriella thought as she continued her walk. She went into the small church. As she entered, she was taken aback by the beautiful paintings which dated back to the sixteenth and fifteenth century. The colours were amazing. Gabriella was mesmerised by its beauty. The feeling that she got from being in this building was hard to explain. Physically she was there, but spiritually she was somewhere else. Gabriella had never felt so at peace.

As she stood there admiring the interior of the church, she suddenly felt the presence of someone else. As she turned around to see who it was, it appeared that no one was there. She was completely alone. Gabriella shrugged it off and continued with her viewing. As Gabriella was about to walk outside she felt a slight breeze on her face. That's strange, she thought, it was a lovely warm day out, no sign of any wind. Outside Gabriella was admiring the bell tower which was constructed much later in the nineteenth century, when all of a sudden the bell let out a small chime.

"No way could that have happened," Gabriella said aloud "this building hasn't been used in years!"

She looked around to see if anyone else was there to see if they had also heard it, but no one was to be seen. Gabriella came to another small building which used to be the monastery's library. A plaque read 'This library used to house a vast collection of important books that were used by many philosophers of that time, but were all destroyed in the war and invasions.' There really wasn't much to look at so she went to find a place to sit and write in her journal.

Gabriella sat by the spring waters that still flow to this day, although you're not allowed to drink the water anymore. Deep in thought, Gabriella wrote about the history and the beauty of the monastery.

"You look troubled," came a voice.

Gabriella looked up. Sat opposite her was a beautiful lady dressed in clothes that were not of this century. Gabriella assumed it was a tour guide dressed in character.

"I don't mean to interrupt you, but I saw you sitting here looking troubled and wondered if I could be of any assistance."

"I'm fine thank you," replied Gabriella, thinking how strange and, to be honest, how rude it was that a complete stranger would just come up and ask if she was troubled!

Gabriella went to walk away.

"Please don't leave, I'm here to help. I know you're confused about a young man in your life and your feelings for him."

Gabriella turned round and looked at the lady. How did she know about Macario, one of the girls must have put her up to it? But as Gabriella looked into her eyes she was totally transfixed.

This total stranger took Gabriella by the hand and sat her down.

"Who are you?" asked Gabriella.

"My name has no importance; I am here to help you to understand why you are having these feelings for this young man. It is your destiny to be together. It will not make any sense to either of you just now but trust me, when two people are meant to be together, and for all the right reasons, the gods will find ways to bring you together."

"What do you mean the gods?" asked Gabriella. "There is only one God."

"Where I am from there are many Gods and Goddesses of which I am one."

Gabriella was now starting to get a bit worried by this person, thinking she was some kind of weirdo, but still, she couldn't take her eyes off her.

"My dear girl, do not be afraid to let your feelings be known, I know much about love, desire and beauty. You were drawn to each other because it is right, you are two beautiful spiritual people that are to be one. When you next meet him you will understand what I am telling you. He has the same concerns as you, but another is helping him to understand, just as I am here to help you."

Gabriella was finding it really hard to understand what was going on. Was there any truth to what this strange but intriguing lady was telling her, or was it just someone playing a very unfunny prank on her?

With that the lady got up, stroked Gabriella's cheek and said, "remember the butterflies, the man in the park, the lady who approached you on the catamaran and the dolphins? They were sent to show you the way to new beginnings."

Gabriella turned away. This was real, no one knew about that except Macario. As Gabriella turned back to say something the lady had gone. She looked around but she had disappeared.

Why do people keep disappearing on me, she thought?

All of a sudden, everyone from her party appeared. It seemed like a dream, one minute she was there all alone then everyone was there.

"Gabriella," called the girls.

"You should have come with us," announced Petra, "it was so beautiful, and the smell of pine from the trees, and the fragrance of all the different flowers was so refreshing."

"Yeah, and no one thought to mention it was another trek uphill!" complained Ingrid.

"Well its one o'clock, I guess we better get back to the coach," suggested Gabriella.

***

Back at the hostel, Joan's birthday buffet was in full swing, they were only allowed two hours so as not to disturb any of the other guests. They were having a really good time, even Gabriella, especially after what she had just experienced. When the party was over they went back to their rooms.

"Let's go out and have some fun, we have a day off tomorrow so no need to be up early," announced Gabriella.

"Sure why not, what did you have in mind?" asked Ingrid.

"I don't know, wherever it leads us!"

After they had showered and changed they headed into the town. They went to a few bars and had something to eat. The nightlife was buzzing in Athens.

"Let's go to a club," said Gabriella, "I feel like dancing."

The other girls thought this was a bit out of character for Gabriella and knew something was bothering her, but they just let her carry on. Once in the club the girls got a drink and found somewhere to sit. As the evening went on, the club was getting busier, and the girls were getting merrier, except for Ingrid who had learnt her lesson from last time!

"Let's hit the dance floor!" shouted Gabriella over the loud music.

They were having a really good time, dancing and singing at the tops of their voices when they were approached by some of the local Greek lads who joined them dancing.

"Would you like a drink?" asked one of the guys.

"No thank you," shouted the girls through the loud music, except for Gabriella.

"I would like a glass of wine please."

"Gabriella what is wrong with you? We don't know these guys. Plus, maybe you've had enough," insisted Martha.

"I feel fine. I'll have this one then we'll go."

As the lad went to get Gabriella's drink, Ingrid followed him, for some reason she didn't trust him. Her intuition was right; she saw him slip something into the glass of wine.

"I'll take that, thank you very much!" Ingrid grabbed the glass from him. "I'm sure the manager and the police will be interested in this?"

With that the lad said something to the other guys and they left pretty quickly. Ingrid informed the manager of what had happened, told the girls, then they left.

When they got back to the hostel Gabriella thanked Ingrid for what she had done.

"If it wasn't for you being intuitive I hate to think what would have happened to me, thank you so much Ingrid." She gave her a huge hug. On that note they all went to bed.

The next morning, the girls woke up around ten o'clock.

"How is everyone feeling this morning, any sore heads?" laughed Ingrid, as she was the only one that didn't really drink the night before. Gabriella seemed to be the one that was suffering a bit.

Martha went and sat on Gabriella's bed.

"Are you ok? You didn't seem to be yourself yesterday, you were fine until we left the monastery, and then wanting to go and get drunk. Did something happen?"

"No I'm fine, I was just letting off a bit of steam, I hadn't intended on getting drunk. I must say I sobered up pretty quick after what that lad did to my drink. How can anyone do something so dangerous? Lucky for me that Ingrid was watching, that could have been some other girl that might not have been so lucky. I shudder to think what could have happened."

"You had a guardian angel watching over you," laughed Martha, "her name being Ingrid!"

Gabriella laughed but thought back to what had happened at the monastery. Someone was definitely watching over her.

The first week passed by very quickly, and the second week was going just as fast. They had two days left and two excursions.

Today the group were off to visit Syntagma square to see the changing of the guards. Formally known as Constitution square, it is the most important square in Athens where Hellenic parliament stands. It is constantly crowded with locals and tourists.

"Ok everyone, listen up!" shouted Susan. "It's getting very crowded now so we need to grab a spot quick so we get a good view."

They all managed to find a place with a good view. As they were waiting for the guards to change, Susan explained a bit about the square.

"The parliament building was originally the royal palace. In 1843, King Otto was forced to grant a constitution to the people of Greece after an uprising during that year, and the square was renamed Syntagma Square. Every solider guards for one hour, three times in total, every forty-eight hours. They have to stand perfectly still until it's time to switch, they work in pairs so they can perfectly coordinate their moves."

The crowds started to go silent as the guards came out to change. They were dressed in their official ceremonial costume. Their uniform has a historic meaning, it refers to the uniform of Kleftes and Amatoloi, two groups of Greek warriors during the war of independence in 1821 against the Ottomans.

"Did you know that the white skirt that they wear has four hundred folds to represent four hundred years of Ottoman occupation over the Greeks?" exclaimed Petra.

"Crikey, that must take a long time to get those folds to look perfect," replied Ingrid.

"I don't think someone sits there folding each fold by hand Ingrid," laughed Petra.

"Each guard is selected according to their height, excellent physical condition and psychological state, as well as character and morality. They train for one month and this includes exercises to keep the body and mind still. They are not allowed to show any facial expressions at all."

"I bet they're fun to be around," Ingrid said sarcastically. "They do look cute though!"

Once the ceremony had finished, they took a walk around the square which boasted a central fountain and a number of statues, as well as a lovely grassy area with trees to relax under, keeping you shaded from the intense heat.

Their last two days were quite relaxed, the visit to the square and a shopping trip into town to end their time in Athens.

"That's it, another country explored," announced Martha. "Onto the next one!"

10

On the plane to Malta, Gabriella was reflecting on her time at the monastery in Athens and what had taken place. The feeling that someone was in the same room as her when there clearly wasn't, the breeze that swept across her face on a hot day when there was no wind, the chime that came from the bell tower that had not been in working order for years, and then the mysterious lady. Am I going mad she thought? I really need to talk to someone about this, but who? I know, Macario. When I get to Malta I will contact him, surly he will understand.

They arrived safely and on time at Malta international airport. They gathered their luggage and boarded the coach for an hour journey to their hostel. The hostel was pleasant with traditional Maltese features, and there was also a very welcoming swimming pool which they had not had at any of the other hostels. Just as well, as the weather was expected to be glorious over the next few weeks.

They were on a night flight so by the time they had checked in and settled into their rooms the day was almost over. They went for a quick something to eat before settling down for the night.

***

After a well-rested night, they all went for breakfast before heading off to the National Museum of Fine Arts. It was an extremely hot day.

"I hope this museum has air-conditioning," complained Ingrid as they got on the coach.

"Can I have everyone's attention please," announced Thomas. "We will be at the museum for approximately one hour, then we will get back on the coach and stop to explore some of the shops and cafes. We will meet up at the exit of the museum at approximately twelve o'clock."

Once in the museum everyone went their own way. Gabriella, Martha, Petra and Ingrid stayed together as usual.

"This looks very nice," said Martha.

"It's a museum, no different to all the other hundreds of museums we have seen," replied Ingrid.

"Well we are in a good mood today," laughed Petra.

"I want to see more exciting things other than museums all the time."

"Come on Ingrid," Gabriella said, putting a comforting arm around her, "Petra can be our commentator for the next hour."

"Great, that really has made me feel a lot better!" grunted Ingrid.

"So, The National Museum of Fine Arts is Malta's major museum for the visual arts. The palace is an historical building built in the 1760s. It used to be the private home of Chavallier Ramon de Sousa y Silva, a wealthy Portuguese knight of the order of St John. The Palace was officially inaugurated as The National Museum of Fine Arts in 1974."

"How riveting."

"Ingrid please, I'm trying to listen, some of us are interested," scowled Martha. "Carry on Petra."

"The works of art that are shown here are by Malta based artist Mattia Preti, who painted the vaulted ceilings of St John Co - Cathedral. His paintings are more of a religious subject opposed to his earlier work of musicians and card players. He established a reputation for his hard work producing art work for churches across the archipelago."

"Across what?" asked Ingrid.

"Archipelago. An extensive group of Islands," replied Petra.

"Next the Italian Artist Caravaggio. He arrived in Malta in 1607 as a fugitive after the papal authority found him guilty of murdering a man in Rome. As you can see his many paintings include: Madonna and child with St Ann, Sleeping Cupid, Supper at Emmaus and the Martyrdom of Saint Matthew. His work provided inspiration throughout the ages, including such masters as Rubens, Velazquez and Rembrandt. He was later imprisoned for fighting, but managed to escape and fled back to Italy where he died two years later at the age of just thirty-nine."

"Sounds like a charming man!" said Ingrid. "It must be time to go now?"

"Last one Ingrid. And finally we have British landscape painter Joseph Mallord William Turner. An English romantic water colourist. You can see the way the soft light captures the colours bringing his paintings to life."

"Really. All I can see are smudges of paint, not capturing me I'm afraid!" Ingrid commented sarcastically.

"If you have finished Ingrid I will continue. Joseph Mallord William Turner entered the Royal Academy of Art schools when he was only fourteen years old, then accepted into the academy a year later. As you can see his work includes: Burning of The House of parliament, The Slave Ship and Rain, Steam and Speed. The Great Western Railway. He was commonly known as 'The painter of light'. So there we have it, an insight to some of the great artists in the world of Art."

"Well done Petra," applauded Martha and Gabriella. "You should take up being a curator, you're so good at it, despite the interruptions!"

"Thanks guys, maybe I have found a new career!" laughed Petra.

Back on the coach Gabriella sat with Ingrid.

"What on earth has gotten into you today? You have not stopped complaining and have been very rude."

"I'm fed up with going to museums all the time, it's so boring."

"So why are you here? You knew what this journey was about, to experience different cultures, including going to museums."

"My parents thought it would do some good, in their words 'to rough it a bit.' I'm more used to sleeping in nice hotels in a comfortable bed, coming and going as I please."

"So you're a spoilt Madame then?! Ingrid sometimes in life we do things that are out of our comfort zones, to teach us that there is more in life than in your case, fancy hotels, which is fine, but it is to also show us that life can be good, fun, exciting with the simple things. Just give it a go, enjoy the time we have on this adventure. Ok the beds may not be the best, there is no room service, but what an experience, you may even surprise yourself!"

"I'll try. Thanks Gabriella, I'll apologise to the other girls."

"Ok people you have two hours to shop and explore," Susan announced. "I know it's not long but we will have plenty more opportunities to shop. When we get back to the hostel you will find information in the lobby of what we will be doing here in Malta for the next two weeks."

Everyone went off in different directions. As Gabriella, Martha, Petra and Ingrid continued on their walk, they came across a market. There were lots of stalls selling all kinds of things: handmade lace, religious artefacts, Maltese glass, and wicker work, pretty much what you would expect really. As they turned into a side street they found a small shop, a silversmiths.

"This looks interesting, let's go in and have a look," said Martha.

As they walked in they were greeted with a happy smiley welcome from the owner who was sitting making pieces of jewellery.

"Good afternoon ladies, feel free to have a look around, if I can be of any assistance please ask."

There wasn't only jewellery but other silverware, like bowls, trinket boxes and money clips.

"Did you make all of these yourself?" asked Gabriella.

"Yes, with the help of my son. We make everything here on the premises so that you can see the work that goes into each piece we make.

"Everything is so beautiful; you can see the love that has gone into making it," replied Gabriella.

Martha purchased some earrings and a matching bracelet, and Gabriella purchased a trinket box. They were starting to feel hungry so went to find a café to have something to eat.

They found a lovely quaint café, and once seated, they looked at the menu and the waitress came to take their order.

Gabriella and Ingrid ordered hobz biz-zeit (an open sandwich of round bread dipped in olive oil, rubbed with ripe tomatoes and filled with a mix of tuna, onion, garlic tomatoes and capers and two glasses of local beer.) Petra ordered Kapunata which was the Maltese version of ratatouille, along with a glass of local wine, and Martha ordered a platter which included: Fazola (butter beans in oil and garlic), Gbejniet tal-bzar (peppered goats cheese), Bigilla (a dip made of mashed beans), a traditional spiced pork sausage, sundried tomatoes, bread dipped in olive oil and a cup of tea.

The food arrived, and it went down a treat.

"That was lovely," exclaimed Petra as she stretched out in her chair. "I could go to sleep now."

"No time for that Petra," laughed Martha. "We have to get to the coach now, you can sleep on the way back!"

When they arrived at the hostel they looked at their agenda for the next two weeks.

"Ok let's see where we are going," announced Gabriella. "We're going to a marine park and swimming with the dolphins, a day's cruise, Medieval Mdina, and our last evening is a night of Maltese Folklore. Sounds great, especially swimming with the dolphins."

"And no more museums?" replied Ingrid.

"No more museums," laughed Gabriella.

Gabriella thought this would be a good time to call Macario. As the others went back to their rooms, Gabriella went and sat outside by the pool. Feeling a little nervous, she dialled his number.

"Gabriella I was just going to call you, we must be tuned in to each other," he laughed. "How are you, and all your adventures?"

"I'm good thank you. The trip is going well, it's been interesting! I wanted to talk to you about something that happened whilst I was in Athens."

Gabriella explained to Macario about the monastery, the strange things that happened and the mysterious lady.

"Macario, she knew all about the stranger in the park, the butterflies and dolphins, the lady that came up to me on the catamaran, only you knew about those things. She said how we were meant to be together and how she was there to help me, and that someone would be there to help you. It was so confusing; can you make any sense of it?"

"Gabriella, when I went on a business trip to Norway recently, I had a strange conversation with this guy telling me how I looked troubled, to not be afraid to show how I feel about you, how we were meant to be together, and how we will know when we see each other. Like you I was transfixed, but I understood what he was saying."

"Macario, that is word for word what the lady told me. This is scaring me now, what is going on?"

"Don't be scared Gabriella, we are meant to be together, I can really see it now. Sometimes things happen that don't make sense, but I guess it's the universe's way of bringing us together through these strange encounters. It doesn't matter how many days, weeks or months you have known someone, they are just numbers. What matters is that we know it's right in our hearts, trust me Gabriella it will all make sense, it is starting to with me."

"I know what you are saying, that's why I had to talk to you, I knew you would make more sense of it, it's just a lot to take in. I am really looking forward to seeing you Macario."

"Me too. Remember if you encounter anything else that you feel is strange and you can't make sense of it, take it as another of God's signs that something wonderful is going to happen! Take care Gabriella, speak to you soon."

Gabriella felt better after talking to Macario but she was still a bit confused.

11

"Good morning ladies and gentlemen. I hope you all have your bathing suits, sun cream and plenty of water? Today is going to be a very hot day," announced Mark. "The coach will be here in a few minutes which will take us to Sliema, where we will board the boat for our day's cruise around Malta. Ok folks, the coach is here, let's go and have a lovely relaxing day on the ocean."

The captain of the boat welcomed all the passengers aboard before sailing off. The sun was beaming down, reflecting off the beautiful blue sea. As they sailed along the coastline, one of the crew gave a commentary about the popular landmarks as they approached them.

"So here you will see The Grand Harbour which is the island's greatest geographic asset. In the distance guarding the entrance on the left is Fort Elmo whilst on the right is Fort Ricasoli. In between you can see two breakwaters with small light houses, which indicate the entrance to Valetta...

We are now approaching St Thomas bay. This is where the locals come to their summerhouses in the summer months, it is very popular due to it being so peaceful and quiet."

"Now this is more like it," sighed Ingrid, "blazing sunshine, blue waters, peace and relaxation."

"Our next landmark is Marsaxlokk. Malta's largest fishing village, surrounded by green vegetation. The fishermen use colourful painted boats called 'Luzzu.' The design is dated back to 800BC when the Phoenicians came to Malta.

There are various stalls daily in the village but the most popular and busiest day is Sunday when the locals flock there to buy their fish and vegetables. There are many fish restaurants along the promenade, the most popular fish in Malta are swordfish and blue fin tuna. Marsaxlolkk bay is one of the most attractive places to visit in Malta."

"Why would anyone want to visit a smelly fish market when you can soak up this wonderful sunshine?" remarked Ingrid.

Gabriella gazed out onto the ocean, the calm sea, the peace and quiet. Her thoughts were with Macario, longing for the time when they would see each other again. Why do you get to me so much Macario, what is it about you?

"The blue grotto and the Dingli cliffs are our next landmarks. The blue grotto is a beautiful natural grotto, it has a number of sea caverns which are extremely popular for diving, and it also featured in the film Troy. The sunlight reflects the fluorescent colours of the submerged flora. When you are close up you can see the orange, purple and green of the minerals in the rocks. I would recommend that you take a boat trip to the blue grotto whilst you're here as you can get up close to the rocks and go through the caverns.

Just ahead we have the Dingli cliffs, a majestic sight from the boat, but also very breathe taking from the cliff top. There is a tiny chapel perched on the edge dedicated to Mary Madgalene."

"This is so beautiful," said Martha. "What a wonderful place Malta is."

"Next is Anchor Bay Popeye village, also known as Sweethaven village, which has a group of rustic and run down wooden buildings, built as a film set for the film 'Popeye'. A two-hundred-foot breakwater was built around Anchor Bay's mouth to protect the set from high seas during filming. Today it is open to the public. It has a number of attractions for visitors, shows, rides and museums."

"Please don't mention museums!" screeched Ingrid. Gabriella and the other girls laughed.

"Finally our last landmark, one of the highlights of the day is the crystal clear waters of the Blue Lagoon in the island of Comino. It is the island's main attraction and one of the best beaches in Malta. It is ideal for swimming, snorkelling and scuba diving or just relaxing on the beach. This beautiful lagoon has been used by film makers for scenes such as 'Swept Away' and 'The Count of Monte Cristo'. We will anchor the boat in the marina-like bay where there will be a buffet lunch for you, then the rest of the afternoon is yours to enjoy before heading back to Sliema."

"This is just fabulous!" exclaimed Petra. "There seems to be a lot of films made here, I'm not surprised it is such a beautiful island. I just love it!"

After lunch the girls went and sat on the beach.

"Who fancies doing a bit of snorkelling?" asked Petra.

"I'll give it a go," replied Ingrid, nervously.

Petra and Ingrid went off snorkelling and Martha laid on the lovely warm sand, sunbathing. Gabriella thought it would be a good time to call her parents.

"Papa it's me, Gabriella."

"Mama, come quickly, Gabriella is on the phone. How are you Bambino? Where are you now? Is everything okay?"

"Slow down papa, everything is fine. I am in Malta, we are on a lovely cruise of the island at the moment, and it is so beautiful here. How are you and mama? Are you busy at the patisserie?"

"We are fine but really missing you Gabriella, the patisserie is very busy, Maria has been a big help, and your brothers have been working hard. Hold on Gabriella, mama wants to talk!"

"Bambino are you okay? I am marking off each day until you come home, are you eating well? Have you been to church?"

"Mama I am fine, yes I am eating well and yes I have been to church! I'm glad Maria is helping you in the patisserie, give her my love. The days are going by so fast mama, I will be home in no time."

"It's not going fast enough for me and papa, Gabriella, we miss you so much."

"I know you do mama; I miss you too. I have to go now though, I will call you when I am in Germany. Love you."

Gabriella loved talking to her parents even though they did worry too much. She did miss home sometimes but was enjoying every minute of her adventures.

"That was great fun," beamed an excited Petra, as she dripped water over Martha and Gabriella.

"Great fun, I don't call nearly drowning great fun Petra!" shrieked a distressed Ingrid.

"Ingrid you only had your face in the water, how could you be drowning!"

Gabriella and Martha laughed, they did find Ingrid's dramatizing funny. They spent the rest of the afternoon soaking up the sun. The day was drawing to an end and the sun was starting to go down. It was time to board the boat back to Sliema then the coach to the Hostel.

***

Back at the hostel Thomas announced that tomorrow was a free day and that some of them were going on a hike if anyone wanted to join them.

"I don't think so," said Ingrid, still trying to get over her snorkelling experience. "I need the day to recover!"

Gabriella, Petra and Martha found the whole thing with Ingrid amusing, they gave her a big hug, all laughing. They were all very tired after being in the sun all day and decided to have an early night.

After a peaceful night's sleep and a good breakfast, the girls were deciding what to do with their day.

"Well seeing that it's Sunday and a day of rest, that is exactly what I am going to do" decided Ingrid. "What are you going to do Gabriella?"

"I am going to find a local church if anyone would like to join me?"

"Why not," Martha exclaimed, "I've not been to church in years, it might do me good!"

"I'll pass thanks," said Petra, "think I will stay here with Ingrid and write some postcards."

Gabriella and Martha looked at the information in the lobby of the hostel for churches. They came across St John Co-Cathedral and decided on that one. After searching through the bus timetable they set off.

As they arrived at the cathedral they stood and admired the exterior. To the right of the building there were three clocks, one showing the time, one showing the day of the week and the other showing the date. In the middle was a balcony and under the balcony, three coats of arms. One was of the Grand Master La Cassiere who paid for the building of the cathedral, one was of Bishop Torres who opened the cathedral, and the third was the coat of arms of religion. The main door was Tuscan.

"Interesting, I wonder how old it is?" enquired Martha.

As they entered the cathedral, they were given a handheld audio guide so they could listen to information about the cathedral. The assistant asked if their intention was to pray whilst on their visit, as there was a designated chapel for this.

"I will be," announced Gabriella.

"Just let a member of staff know when you are ready and they will guide you to the chapel," replied the assistant.

"Wow, you would not think, looking from the outside, how beautiful and colourful it is inside, it's stunning!" whispered Martha. "Just look at this patchwork marble floor!"

As they walked through the cathedral, admiring the paintings, sculptures and tapestries, they listened to their audio guide.

"One of the greatest treasures here in the cathedral is a huge painting of John the Baptist, by the artist Caravaggio. But his most famous work is the painting depicting 'The Beheading of Saint John the Baptist.' This was considered one of Caravaggios masterpieces and the only painting signed by him.
You will also see paintings by Mattia Preti illustrating events from the life of John the Baptist.

The cathedral contains eight chapels of St John, dedicated to the patron saint of the eight languages of the knights. On the left side of the church are the following chapels:

The chapel of the Anglo Bavarian Langue, formally known as the chapel of the relic where the knights used to keep relics that they had required through the centuries.

The chapel of Provence, dedicated to Saint Michael.

The chapel of France, dedicated to the conversion of Saint Paul.

The chapel of Italy, dedicated to Saint Catherine, the patron saint of the Italian section.

And the chapel of Germany, dedicated to the epiphany of Christ.

To your right you have:

The chapel of Blessed Sacrament, which was formally known as the chapel of our lady of Rhodes.

The chapel of Auvergne, dedicated to Saint Sebastian.

The chapel of Aragon, dedicated to Saint George.

And finally, the chapel of Castile, Leon and Portugal, dedicated to James the Greater.

As we enter the nave, another impressive feature in the church is its collection of marble tombstones where important knights were buried."

"This place is amazing," Martha commented. "The work that has gone in to it, it is covered from ceiling to floor with such beautiful art. I would have never thought I would enjoy walking around a church so much!"

Gabriella smiled at Martha.

"Martha, I'm going to find the assistant to take me to the chapel of prayer, are you going to come?"

"You know what? I think I will Gabriella."

The assistant led them to the chapel of prayer. It was so quiet you could hear a pin drop. Gabriella and Martha sat in one of the pews for a few moments then knelt to pray. After about twenty minutes Gabriella turned to see if Martha was okay, and saw that she was crying. Gabriella gently squeezed Martha's hand. When they had finished they got up and quietly left the chapel and went outside. Gabriella put her arms around Martha and gave her a long hug enquiring if she was okay.

"Well I don't know where that came from," Martha blurted. "I was fine one minute and the next I was in floods of tears.

"It was the Holy Spirit touching your heart Martha, releasing all that you have been holding on to."

"When I think about it, I guess I have been holding on to a lot of stuff recently. I must say, I do feel lighter and quite uplifted. Thank you for inviting me today."

The girls went for a coffee before heading back to the hostel.

"How was church?" asked Petra.

"Very uplifting, inspiring, and spiritual!" beamed Martha.

"Well you certainly look happy. If that's how church makes you feel I think I will come next time," joked Ingrid.

"St Johns co-cathedral is an amazing church; you really need to go to see what I mean. It would do you good Ingrid!" added Martha.

"So what have you two been up to, or do I dare ask?" Gabriella enquired.

"Nothing much, writing post cards, listening to Ingrid being a drama queen and complaining as normal!"

"Excuse me!" bellowed Ingrid. "I am here you know!"

They all roared with laughter.

The rest of the day and evening was spent relaxing.

12

"What another glorious day it is, a perfect day for swimming with the dolphins, I have always wanted to do this," pointed out an excited Petra. "Did you know they consume up to thirty pounds of fish per day? They are known to help assist in healing people with disabilities or trauma, especially children, and also assist with those with some forms of depression. How amazing is that? What beautiful, intelligent, spiritual creatures they are!"

"Have you swallowed the encyclopaedia again Petra?" mocked Ingrid.

"Okay ladies, let's go and meet the others!" Gabriella encouraged them out of the door.

At the Mediterraneo Marine Park they were all given an information guide.

"For those of you that are swimming with the dolphins, we need to make our way there now," announced Susan. "Thomas and I will be assisting you, Mark and Clare will join those that are not swimming in the spectator's area."

"Good morning ladies and gentlemen, welcome to Mediterraneo Marine Park. Before we get you in the water with the dolphins we would like you to watch this short documentary explaining a bit about them and the training that they are given, then we will get you in your wet suits."

"How exciting!" beamed Petra.

After they had watched the documentary, they were split into two groups, Susan with one half and Thomas with the other. They were led to the pool where the dolphins and their trainers were waiting.

Jennifer the trainer invited the ten in her group into the water where they were greeted by a beautiful bottlenose dolphin named Onda who was waving her flippers, her way of saying hi! Jennifer explained that Onda and the other dolphins in the park are trained through the positive reinforcement technique which stimulates them both physically and mentally. By blowing a whistle or a bridge as the trainers called it, indicated that the dolphin had the correct behaviour and therefore received a reward. They would be fed a mixture of capelin, sprat and herring.

Gabriella, Martha, Ingrid and Petra were waiting eagerly in the pool for Onda to do some tricks and to be able to interact with her. Once Jennifer started making hand gestures, Onda started to do spins, flips, balancing a ball on her nose and retrieving hoops. Then it was the girls turn. Onda swam up to them as they lined up. One at a time they gave Onda a stroke on the head, a kiss on her nose, then in turn they held on to her fin as she pulled them along. Ingrid was a bit unsure and needed some encouragement.

"Come on Ingrid you can do it, just hold on, there's nothing to be scared of," shouted Martha.

"Okay, here goes" shrieked Ingrid as she held onto Onda's fin.

"Wow that was exhilarating, I want to do it again!"

The girls laughed with joy and gave Ingrid a big hug. It was time for them to leave the pool so Jennifer could prepare Onda for the next group.

As the girls got changed, they were still chatting excitingly about their experience with Onda.

"That was probably one of the best experiences I have ever had!" Ingrid blurted out.

"Don't say you're going all soft on us," laughed Petra

"Petra don't be so childish," Ingrid replied.

"And she's back!" mocked Petra.

The whole group moved on to see the sea lions perform. The sea lions were trained in the same way as the dolphins, allowing them to perform in front of an audience without the need of any form of restraint. They balanced balls on their noses, and pretended to play a trumpet. They would even smack a trainer with their fin when the trainer's back was turned, and then start clapping. It was all very amusing and everyone was in fits of laughter.

Sea lions live for approximately thirty years. There were three sea lions at the marine park. Dana, Junior and Joey. Junior was the first of the sea lions to be born in Malta, and he now weighed about two hundred and forty pounds.

After a very entertaining performance they moved on to see the parrots, cockatoos, macaws and reptiles before ending their day at the marine park.

***

Back at the hostel, Gabriella, Ingrid, Martha and Petra were still talking about their experiences swimming with Onda the dolphin.

"It is certainly something I will never forget," said Petra.

They all agreed. Just then, Gabriella received a text message from Macario.

'Hi Gabriella. Hope you are okay and have settled after your encounter in Athens!? And enjoying your time in Malta. I have been very busy, went to Lisbon to see about possibly opening a restaurant there. Really missing you and counting the days till we see each other in Paris. Macario x'

"Well somebody has brought a smile to your face," exclaimed Ingrid. "Would that someone be a certain Macario?"

Gabriella could feel her face redden, but just laughed it off, thinking of when they would meet again.

There was only one day left in Malta. Tomorrow was their last day of excursions and they had a lot to fit in. A trip to Medieval Mdina, Mosta Dome, Ta' Qali craft village and then the Maltese Folklore night.

"Good morning everyone. I hope you all had a good night's sleep?" enquired Mark. "We have a packed-filled day, so make sure you have a good breakfast and are ready to board the coach at nine thirty."

After breakfast the girls went back to their room to collect their rucksacks and then boarded the coach for their visit to Mdina.

Once they arrived the coach stopped in front of the city gate situated on a hill in the centre of the island, where they all descended.

"We will be staying here for two hours," announced Clare. "Please take an information leaflet. If we could all meet back here at midday so we can continue on to our next stop."

The gate to the entrance took you across a bridge overlooking a dry moat. It was like taking you into another world. There was a warren of narrow winding streets with shops and cafes.

"This place is beautiful," exclaimed Martha. "Just look at these buildings, the architecture is amazing. According to the information, they're made from the local sandstone, look at the honey colour of them. Also if you noticed those gates that we came through, well they date back to the knights of Malta."

"Careful Martha, you're starting to sound like Petra!" Ingrid warned her, slightly giggling.

Gabriella could not help but laugh.

The more they walked around, the more interesting the buildings became. They all looked pretty much the same, but each one had its own uniqueness about it. Mdina was an enclosed city with very few residents, small in size but rich in history.

"Can you believe that people actually live here?" added an intrigued Petra. "Have you noticed there's no traffic passing through, only a horse drawn carriage is used for the tourists?"

"But how do the residents get around when they want to go out of the city?" asked a puzzled Ingrid.

"The residents have cars; they are the only ones that are allowed to drive through here. That's why it's known as the silent city."

They came across a lovely café called Fontanella, where they stopped and had coffee and cake.

"It has a very peaceful, relaxing atmosphere here and so clean."

"I think I could live here," said Martha.

"I know what you're saying," agreed Petra.

"Are you two mad? Why would you want to live in a place that's so sterile with hardly any people?" Ingrid grunted.

"Ingrid, are you ever happy about anything?" replied an angry Martha.

"What, I was only saying!"

"Well don't."

Gabriella gave Ingrid a stern look.

"Why don't we go and have a look at the view from the viewing area before we go?" suggested Gabriella.

The view across Malta was breath taking. It gave you an idea of just how small Malta was. After a peaceful tour around Mdina, they moved on to their next destination, Mosta Dome, the most impressive church in Malta.

"This will be a short visit to the church," explained Mark. "It really will be a quick look around."

"Well, what's the point then?" complained Ingrid.

"I thought you was going to stop all of this?" whispered Gabriella.

"Sorry, but I really don't see the point!"

Gabriella just raised her eyes up to the heavens.

Once inside the church, Petra did her normal narrating, unaware that everyone in their group was listening.

"Mostra Dome was built in 1860 with its massive rotunda (a round building with a dome). Some say it is the third largest in the world. During the Second World War, the church was almost destroyed during an air raid when a bomb fell through the dome without exploding. At the time, a morning mass was in progress where three hundred people attended, but amazingly no one was hurt."

"Oh my word, that must have been really scary. God certainly was watching over them!" proclaimed Gabriella.

Petra continued.

"The army took the bomb outside and diffused it. A replica was made, as you can see, and is now a famous tourist attraction."

"Thank you Petra, that was very informative," responded Mark.

Petra turned around and realised everyone had been listening to her.

"What just happened? Why didn't you tell me they were all listening?" Petra said, feeling slightly embarrassed.

"Okay folks, I said this had to be a quick one, let's get back on the coach and move on to Ta' Qali crafts village, it's only open for the next two hours," explained Mark.

The Ta' Qali craft village was located in a former RAF wartime air field, and was a very popular tourist attraction. Everything that was made there was made by local experts. There were all different kinds of crafts. Clay pots and bowls, ceramics, glass ornaments and jewellery. Everything was beautifully made.

They all bought something for friends and family as this was the last place for them to purchase anything before they had to leave Malta.

After a rushed look around it was back on the coach, and back to the hostel to get ready for their final evening out.

The girls were having a glass of wine in their room whilst getting ready.

"This Maltese Folklore night sounds like it's going to be fun," smiled Ingrid.

Gabriella, Martha and Petra just looked at each other, then at Ingrid.

"Did you just use the word fun?" mocked Petra.

"Come on guys, I'm not that bad. Am I!?"

"Give her another drink before she turns back into Ingrid," laughed Martha.

As they arrived at the Folklore evening they were greeted by waiters with a welcome drink before being escorted to their table. As there were so many it was twelve to a table. Clare and Thomas sat on the girls table and Susan and Mark sat with the others on another table. The band was playing in the back ground.

"Ladies and gentlemen, welcome to the Maltese Folklore Night," announced the manager. "Before our entertainment starts for the evening, I invite you all to please go to our buffet where you will be served some of Malta's finest foods. If you could go one table at a time that will save big queues. I hope you enjoy your evening. Thank you."

They were halfway through the tables when it was the girls table to go up.

There was so much to choose from. Anti pasti, barbeque chicken, baked macaroni, stuffed marrow, Mediterranean fish in tomato and caper sauce, roast potatoes and vegetables, bean salad, and the list could go on. They all had a bit of whatever they could fit on to their plate.

On each table there was stone baked Maltese bread dipped in an authentic olive oil, bottles of water and a mixture of red and white wine. Any extra drink after that was at an additional charge.

When the main course had finished it was time for deserts and coffee. As people were finishing their food, the local dance team was preparing for the night's entertainment.

"That was delicious, I enjoyed every mouthful of that," blurted a very full Petra.

They all nodded their heads in agreement.

First up to get people in the mood was a local mandolin player, who entertained everyone with a melody of Maltese music. All the locals were singing along and those that didn't understand what he was saying still joined in, clapping and dancing in their seats.

Martha, Petra, Ingrid and Gabriella were all having a wonderful time. After a few more drinks it was time for the local dance team to perform. It was all in full swing. Dressed in traditional Maltese costume, the dancers performed the Maltese Frejgatina, otherwise known as the fisherman's dance which included a bit of audience participation. The dancers were pulling people out of the audience to join them in their dance, except for Ingrid who volunteered herself.

"Come on girls!" Ingrid beckoned the others to get up and dance. "This is fun."

Everyone on their table got up and joined in, even their tour guides, Susan, Mark, Thomas and Clare.

After the dance performance had finished, everyone went back to the tables whilst the dancers had a break.

"I wonder what's coming up next. I want to dance!" said an excited and slightly drunk Ingrid.

The dancers were ready to come back out; they had changed costume for the next dance. This time they were going to perform the farmers dance. The music started and everyone waited for them to begin. It was another fun, lively dance and everyone was enjoying it, then all of a sudden they brought out some donkeys.

"What the!" gasped Ingrid. "Donkeys! Don't tell me they're going to dance?"

Gabriella, Martha and Petra could not stop laughing at Ingrid.

"Wait for it… and there she goes!" roared Petra.

Ingrid started dancing with the dancers and tried to sit on one of the donkeys. Everyone was cheering and clapping which only encourage Ingrid to do it more. After the dancers had rescued the poor donkey from Ingrid, they politely escorted her back to her table.

"Ingrid you're barmy," laughed Martha.

"I know!" she replied, reaching for another glass of wine to drink.

The night was coming to a close, and everyone had had such a good evening and a few too many wines! But it was time to go as they had a plane to catch the following day. They were expecting a few sore heads in the morning!

13

On the flight to Germany there were quite a few tired looking and hungover passengers! Even the tour guides Mark, Thomas, Clare and Susan were looking a bit jaded.

"I thought I asked you guys to not let me drink like that again," Ingrid whispered as she lifted her dark glasses.

"That's the only time you don't actually complain, or act like a drama queen," Petra pointed out. "You are quite funny, and if I dare say it, a joy to be around!"

"Well thanks Petra, it's nice to know you think so highly of me!"

"My pleasure Ingrid."

Eventually they all drifted off to sleep for the entire journey.

They arrived at Berlin Tegel airport with a bit of a bump, which jolted awake those who were still sleeping.

"What's wrong with these pilots?" moaned a grumpy Ingrid. "Don't they know how to land a plane properly?"

Once they were off the plane and had got their luggage, they boarded the coach to take them to their hostel.

When they got to the hostel, Clare announced that the rest of the day was to do what they wanted, but reminded them that the following morning would be an early start for their first trip to Fernsehturm (the Berlin TV tower). Most people stayed in their rooms and rested after the late night they had the day before.

The next morning everyone was up bright and early, ready for breakfast. There were a variety of different foods to choose from: eggs, bacon, sausage, smoked fish, a selection of cheese, pancakes, sweet buns, croissants, bread, rolls, cereal, juice and coffee.

"That was very nice, nothing like a full tummy to start the day!" declared Martha.

When everybody was ready, they made their way to reception, where Mark, Clare, Thomas and Susan were waiting.

"Listen up everyone," yelled Clare. "Today we will be taking the train to Berlin Alexanderplatz station, then a short walk to the Berlin TV tower so please stay close. If we are all ready, let's go."

When they arrived at the Berlin Alexanderplatz station, the TV tower was directly opposite. Once inside, everyone had to go through a security check. Susan went to the information point to get the information leaflets and handed them out. They took the elevator in two goes as it only took ten people at a time up to the observation platform.

"Ok you all have your information leaflets," announced Susan. "There is no need for us to go around the tower together. We will stay here for one hour then meet downstairs at the information point, so keep an eye on the time."
"Let's go and have a look at the views," said Martha.

"Wow, breath-taking. It's such a clear day, you can see right across the city," added Petra. "According to the information leaflet, you can see The Reichstag which is the parliament building, the Brandenburg Gate, the Olympic Stadium, the Museum Island and Potsdam square."

"So lady of information, can you actually point out where these places are?" demanded a sarcastic Ingrid.

"Well, no, not really. I'm just telling you what the information is saying," replied Petra. But I'm sure I can find some who can. Wait one minute and I'll be back."

She hurried off to find someone, and was back in a flash.

"Okay. This is Hans, one of the staff here." Petra introduced him to the others. "He is going to show us where these places are, so Ingrid pay attention!"

Hans showed the girls where each place was at every point of the compass. He also told them a bit of the history of the tower.

"The TV tower is the city's tallest building, standing at three hundred and sixty-eight meters high. It was constructed between 1965 and 1969. The tower illustrated that a better future was being built in East Berlin. It is one of the most popular attractions for tourists in Berlin with one of the best views. As the tower is such a popular place to visit for safety reasons the maximum number of visitors at one time for both floors is three hundred and twenty. On the floor above, there is the rotating restaurant which makes one revolution every thirty minutes. The restaurant gets very busy, so I would recommend you book a table if you are planning to eat here."

"I hope this has been helpful ladies? Enjoy the rest of your time here at the tower and in Berlin."

"Thank you for your time and information you gave us Hans, it was very helpful," Petra replied.

"Shall we go and have a look at this rotating restaurant?" Ingrid enquired.

It was still early so nobody was actually eating as of yet, so they were allowed to have a quick look around the restaurant.

"Okay, I can't feel us moving." Ingrid pointed out.

"That's the idea, if it moved too fast it would probably make you feel sick, especially if you're eating," explained Petra. "It is a slow and gentle rotation."

"Look at the time, we had better meet the others," announced Martha.

"There are a few shopping malls around Alexanderplatz," informed Clare. "We thought you may like to do a little shopping whilst we're here, again, you have our mobile numbers if you need to call one of us. You have two hours then we will meet back here before getting the train back to the hostel."

"Now that sounds more like it, shopping - my favourite hobby!" exclaimed an excited Ingrid.

The first building that stood out to a lot of them was the Alexa, a highly visible, pink concrete shopping mall. The Alexa is one of Berlin's largest shopping malls.

"This looks interesting, let's go in here!" shrieked Ingrid.

"Don't go mad Ingrid, we still have Paris yet!" joked Petra.

Gabriella couldn't wait for Paris, only a few more weeks until she could see Macario and her brother, Michael.

The girls spent ages in and out of the shops trying to restrain Ingrid from buying everything! After another half hour they went to the food court to eat.

Gabriella and Martha chose the currywurst - a large sausage cut into thick slices, seasoned with a spicy ketchup and a generous amount of curry powder, served with French fries. Petra had bratkaryoffein - fried potatoes with diced bacon and onions, and Ingrid chose schweinshaxe - a crispy grilled pork hock with sauerkraut.

"It feels good to sit down, all that shopping, well, window shopping, has made me hungry," Gabriella remarked. "I thought the clothes shop with the two entrances, a large one for the adults and a small one of the children, was so cute."

"Yes, it was," laughed Martha. "There sure are a lot of shops to look around, all five floors full!"

"Now that's what I call an ideal day out," grinned Ingrid.

When they had finished their food they made their way back to the TV Tower to meet the others, then back to the hostel.

"Before you all disappear," announced Thomas, "the schedule for our time here will be on the notice board in the next hour, so please have a look so you know where we're going and at what time."

Whilst they were all relaxing in their rooms, Gabriella's phone rang, it was her mother.

"Mama are you ok, what's wrong?" asked a worried Gabriella.

"Nothing is wrong Bella, I wanted to tell you some very exciting news. Mario and Charlotte are expecting a baby, I'm going to be a Nona again and your father a Nonno!"

"That's fantastic news mama, tell Mario and Charlotte I'm really happy for them. Are you and papa okay?"

"We are fine Bella, counting the days till you come home, not long now! We miss you so much. Are you having a good time?"

"I miss you too mama. Yes, I'm having a brilliant time, we're in Germany now. I will have lots to tell you when I get back. Mama this call is costing you a lot, give my love to papa and everyone, I will call you when I am in Paris. Love you."

"Good news?" enquired Petra.

"Yes! My brother Mario and his wife Charlotte are expecting a baby, this will be their fourth, so I am going to be an auntie again."

"Congratulations!" yelled the girls as they gave Gabriella a big hug.

They spent the rest of the day chatting about everything and anything. Later that evening, Martha went to see their schedule. Tomorrow's trip was to the Berlin Wall and a food and street tour.

***

"Good morning to you all. I hope you had a restful night?" Thomas enquired. "So today's trip is to the famous Berlin Wall which will take approximately one hour, we will then be going on to Kreuzberg food and street tour, where we will be able to sample some of the local foods. So if we can all board the coach now, we can set off."

When they reached the stop point at the Berlin Wall they were met by their guide Bernard.

"Guten Morgen. Good morning. Welcome to Berlin. Today I will be giving you a brief history of the Berlin Wall and showing you where it stood. If you would like to follow me."

"Here you can see a row of cobbled stones, this is the footprint of where the wall stood but if we walk further down, you will see that part of the wall still stands, a symbol of the triumph of freedom."

"Why was it built in the first place?" asked Martha.

"It was built to divide West Berlin to East Berlin. East Germany was backed by the soviets at the time, whilst the U.S backed West Germany. The East claimed that the wall was to stop Western spies from entering, but it was actually built to stop residents from deflecting to the West. Even the subway system that ran across Germany was divided after the wall was built. It was a tangible symbol of the suppression of human rights during the cold war."

"Why was it called the cold war?" enquired Ingrid.

"It was the name that was given to the relationship between the USA and USSR after World War II, a state of political and military tension, a coldness between too powerful countries."

"That's just it, it's all about who can be more powerful than the other, why can't everyone just get on, then none of these conflicts and wars would happen," snapped Petra.

"So when was it built?" added Gabriella.

"Construction of the wall began on the 13th of August 1961 when East German soldiers put up miles of barbed wire which was later replaced with concrete slabs. It eventually grew into an intricate border security system riddled with many trenches, floodlights, patrol roads, electric fence, attack dogs and watch towers staffed by guards. During its time, one hundred and thirty-six people died trying to cross the wall."

"The wall was up until a surprise announcement was made in November 1989, that all travel restrictions to the West would be lifted, border controls still existed but were less strict until July 1999 when all Berlin wall border controls ended. Finally, the wall came down and Germany became one country again."

"What an awful time it must have been," said Martha.

"Yes it was," replied Bernard. "It has left many scars mentally, but Germany can at last get on with a better life now. Are there any more questions? In that case, our tour has come to an end. I hope you have more of an understanding of what happened. Enjoy the rest of your stay in Berlin. Auf Wiedersehen. Goodbye."

"You read about these things but you can never understand what it must have really been like for these people, but being here makes you feel more compassionate of the situation," Gabriella added.

When back on the coach they headed to the Kreuzberg food and street tour. As they got to their destination, they were once again greeted by a tour guide.

"Hallo, welcome to the Kreuzberg food and street tour. My name is Hilda and I will be your guide. There is only one way we start the food tour here in Berlin and that is with a currywurst, if you have not experienced a currywurst before, it is a fried pork sausage cut into slices and seasoned with a curry ketchup. Very delicious."

Gabriella and Martha had already tasted a currywrust but it was Petra and Ingrid's first time. Petra enjoyed it, but Ingrid was not so keen.

Once they had finished their currywurst, Hilda went on to explain about the annual water and vegetable battle.

"The water and vegetable battle is an event that takes place every year since 1998. It is a battle of two neighbourhood districts, Friedrichshain and Kreuzberg which are separated by the Oberbaum Bridge. Known as Gemueseschlacht, the two neighbourhoods gather their weapons of rotten foods, flour and water guns and then hurl the food at each other, pushing the other team back to their side of the bridge in an effort to gain control of the bridge. It does get extremely messy so people who don't want to take part are advised to avoid the bridge."

"Why on earth would anyone want to throw rotten food at each other, it must stink?" replied Ingrid pretending to gag.

"Because it's what they do, having fun!" Petra added.

"I can think of much better ways to have fun than being hit with rotten vegetables!" Ingrid pointed out.

Moving onto the busy streets of Kretzberg you could smell the aromas of spices as you passed the Turkish spice shops. Kretzberg is a vibrant multicultural area, where one third of their residents are not German. You can find almost anything in this one place.

"So who would like to sample a rollmop?" smiled Hilda. "A pickled herring in other words. Here in Berlin it is an old time finger food that you can eat in one bite."

They all gave it a try except for Ingrid.

"Go on Ingrid, we've all done it, it's not that bad," informed Martha.

"Ok," agreed a reluctant Ingrid.

Ingrid popped a rollmop into her mouth and spat it straight back out.

"I have never tasted anything so disgusting, that was vile!" Ingrid spluttered.

"Okay, let's move on," laughed Hilda. "As you can see we have an array of different shops and food stands, cafes, beer halls and even a few mosques. Kreuzberg is also known for its street art which you will see as we go further along, but first another food tasting."

"Oh no, hope it's better than the last one," complained Ingrid.

"Next we are going to stop at one of the many Turkish stands where you can taste their lovely roasted nuts and dried fruits."

As they gathered around the stand, they were handed out a small container each with different roasted nuts, some spicy some not spicy and some dried fruits.

"Now these are delicious, I'm going to buy some of these," said a delighted Ingrid.

"Thank goodness for that," Petra replied sarcastically.

The next stand was giving out samples of wostok, a German lemonade, which was very refreshing. As they continued their tour they arrived at the amazing street art.

"Now we come to SO36 with its colourful street art. There are some well-known artists that have left their mark here on the city, like international urban artists Roa from Belguim, Blu from Italy and Banksy from the United Kingdom, plus some of our own local artists."

"Wow, phenomenal murals," commented Gabriella. "So much talent in one place, it must be so satisfying to be able to paint a masterpiece like that, I do admire them."

"So our last stop of the day is the beer hall, you can't leave Kreuzberg without having a glass of Kloster, our traditional German beer."

After they had finished their beer they thanked Hilda then headed back to the coach. When they reached the hostel they looked at their agenda for the following day before calling it a night, a very early night for Gabriella, Ingrid, Martha and Petra.

14

The following morning after breakfast, they headed out to what was going to be an emotional excursion to the Sachsenhausen Concentration Camp. On the coach Thomas relayed to everyone that this was not going to be one of the most exciting tours, but probably the most important one of the whole journey. A very informative tour that may upset some people.

At the Concentration camp they were led to the gate by their guide Hendrik. As you walked through the entrance gate the slogan, 'ARBEIT MACHTERE', meaning work means freedom, was maliciously hung. This was on many of the entrance gates of the concentration camps. You could see the original wall where prisoners would have been marched past or taken by truck before going through the main gate, where all prisoners were then interrogated. Sachsenhausen is just one of the camps that is open to the public, it stands as a reminder of the darkest days of Berlin's history.

Hendrik began his talk.

"As the first purpose-built camp established under Himmler, Sachsenhausen was conceived as a model structure with a view to subjecting prisoners to the absolute power of the SS. In 1936, as the summer Olympics were going on, prisoners were sent from Estervangan camp to build Sachsenhausen. The high walls and barbed wire electric fences hid the horrific program from the rest of the world. By 1945, fifteen thousand concentration camps were built throughout Europe."

"Fifteen thousand!" gasped Martha.

"As we go by the buildings, you will see what sort of conditions the prisoners were subject to. Most of the buildings are reconstructions but there are still some original buildings. The run down green building just to the side of us was known as the Green Monster, the mess hall of the SS officers. As a punishment, knowing that the prisoners were starving and not allowed any of the food, they were made to cook and serve the officers."

"They certainly were monsters," raged Petra, "how can you be so cruel?"

"Here we have some of the original barracks for prisoners. This one to your left was like a prison within a prison, it has its own wall with barbed wire on the top, where enemy officers were kept and tortured. As we move along you can see there are several barracks, each one was built to hold one hundred and forty inmates, but four hundred were crammed into the wooden hovels instead. As we go in you can see that each barrack has a single wash room containing seven toilets, again, that would be shared by the four hundred inmates."

"How disgusting," Ingrid muttered under her breath.

"We now come to the execution trench, if we go down into the trench you will see where prisoners would be lined up one by one and shot, others were led into this closed area where there were SS doctors dressed in white coats. It would give the impression that the prisoners were going to have a medical examination, but instead, once inside the room, they would be tortured and shot. All the prisoners would have their heads shaved and forced to wear striped uniforms which were numbered. This was to rob them of any individuality. All the buildings looked pretty much the same, very drab and dingy with as little as possible in them making the inmates feel less worthy."

"Makes you think how much we worry about the way we look today, isn't that right Ingrid!" remarked Petra sarcastically.

"The concentration camps were used for slave labour. Work brought death to many of the inmates who were abused and underfed. On the parade ground, prisoners stood for hours, morning and night, day after day, no matter what the weather was like, waiting for barrack role calls. The camp was made into a triangular shape so that the guards could see from every angle from their watchtowers. The whole camp was protected by electric fences, making any attempted escape impossible, but desperate inmates would commit suicide by throwing themselves onto the wire mesh. Thousands of people died during this horrific time.

In April 1945, the three thousand frail and sick prisoners that were left behind in Sachsenhausen were eventually liberated by the Russians. Many were so diseased, malnourished and exhausted that they died during their first few weeks of freedom. But for those that did survive would be a time that would never be forgotten. Remember, it was not only the Jews that were subjected to persecution, it was groups such as gypsies, homosexuals and Jehovah witnesses. In 1990 it was made sure that every prisoner was mentioned and remembered."

"We have now come to the end of our tour. Are there any questions?" asked Hendrik. "Then I would like to thank you for coming today and sharing this, not so pleasant experience and hope that you have gained more knowledge and understanding of what went on in those horrific times."

As everyone got back on the coach it was silent, not one word was spoken until they arrived back at the hostel.

"Before you all go," announced Clare, "I just wanted to say, today has been an eye opener for all of us, what we heard and experienced is something I know I will never forget. The next few days will be free days to do as you wish before our last visit to the Brandenberg Gate."

"That was awful," said Martha. "All those poor people, what they went through, how can human beings be so cruel to each other?"

"You see films and read books about these things, but being there is just something else altogether" added Gabriella. "How they must have suffered, it's so sad."

"It's barbaric," replied Petra.

For once Ingrid was quiet, no sarcastic comments were made, she just sat there in silence. This was certainly one place that none of them would ever forget.

After their few days of rest and relaxation it was on to the Brandenberg Gate.

As the area was closed to all traffic, the coach parked up and everyone walked down to the gate.

"Here we have one of the most well-known landmarks in Germany," announced Susan. "The Brandenberg Gate which was built in 1791. It was designed by architect Carl Gotthad Langhans and inspired by the Acropolis in

Athens. The construction was ordered by King Friedrich Wilhelm II as a symbol of peace, and was the main entrance into the city. The king felt it most important in the Prussian empire, but he died before it was complete.

The gate stands at twenty-eight meters high and sixty-five and a half meters wide. As you can see on top of the gate, the beautiful statue of the famous chariot guided by four horses and driven by Victoria, the Roman goddess of victory. It is best known as the Quadriga. In 1806 it was stolen by Napoleon Bonaparte and kept in Paris until its return to Berlin in 1814 upon Napoleons defeat."

"Originally, only the royal family was allowed to walk through the centre of the arch of the gate, everyone else had to walk through the other arches. In 1933, Hitler came to power, and was appointed the position of chancellor. That evening he was treated to a torchlight procession through Berlin where Stormtroopers and SS members passed under the Brandenberg Gate to the presidential palace. The German Democratic Republic incorporated the gate into the Berlin Wall, closing it off and making Brandenberg a symbol of division in the city. In 1989 the gate reopened."

"Here we stand on Pariser Platz. Before World War II, Pariser Platz was the grandest square in Berlin, flanked by American and French embassies, the finest hotel, The Adion, and the Academy of arts. In the last few years of the war, all the buildings around the square were turned into rubble by the air raids and heavy artillery bombardment. The only structure left standing was the Brandenburg Gate. When the city was reunited in 1990, the Pariser Platz was made into a fine urban space again, the embassies, the hotel and the arts academy were reinstated and prestigious firms would be encouraged to build around the square."

"There we have it, a piece of history of the Brandenburg gate. If you want to have a wander around and take photos, we will be here for the next thirty minutes before we head back to the hostel."

Gabriella, Ingrid, Petra and Martha went and sat by the fountain after taking their photos.

"You just can't imagine what went on here," Martha said. "All of the soldiers marching through the gate, Hitler giving out his orders, I would love to know what went on behind those closed doors."

"Nothing very pleasant I would imagine," replied Ingrid.

"No I guess not."

They headed back to the hostel to spend their last few hours getting packed before heading off to the airport to their last destination, Paris. Just before they were leaving Gabriella received a text from Macario.

'Really looking forward to seeing you in Paris. Let me know when you arrive and what free days you have and I will arrange to be there at that time. Until then. Macario xxx'

Gabriella smiled, feeling the excitement in her tummy longing to see Macario again, and of course her brother Michael.

15

"Bonjour, and welcome to Paris," announced the stewardess. "We hope you had a comfortable flight and look forward to you flying with us again."

"Ahh, Gay Paree!" Ingrid blurted out in her worse French accent. "I do love Paris; they have the most wonderful boutiques here."

"Ingrid we're not here just to shop, we're here to educate ourselves," Petra pointed out.

"I am educating myself, with the French fashion!" Ingrid replied.

"Come on girls, let's get our bags and get on the coach," laughed Gabriella and Martha.

At the hostel they were greeted by their hosts, Emmanuel and Sasha.

"Welcome to Paris, we hope you enjoy your stay with us and touring around our beautiful city. When you have unpacked, we have laid on a small buffet for you before you retire for the evening."

Once they had unpacked, everyone made their way to the communal lounge where they helped themselves to some food.

"This is very nice," smiled Martha. "You don't normally get this in a hostel."

"I think it's because it's late, and there are so many of us, and we haven't eaten! They are just being kind; it won't be like that every evening!" laughed Petra.

"Ladies and gentlemen, if I could have your attention please," shouted Thomas. "Before we retire for the night, I just wanted to say that as this is our last destination before heading back home to our own countries, there will be more time for you to relax and explore by yourselves. Tomorrow I will give you the days and times of our excursions whilst we are here, there won't be too many. We will meet at ten o'clock in the morning for breakfast and I will let you know then what our day will consist of. Have a restful sleep and see you in the morning."

Everyone was feeling rather tired; it had been a long day so they all went to bed.

***

"Morning everyone, I hope you had good sleep," Clare began. "Our trip this morning will be to the very famous Louvre Museum where we will spend a few hours, then we will take a fifteen to twenty-minute walk to Notre Dame. Are there any questions? No? Okay, once we have had breakfast we will meet outside ready to take the coach to the Louvre."

"Really," complained Ingrid. "I didn't think we would do any more museums. Why would anyone want to spend a few hours looking at old paintings and statues when there are so many other beautiful things to see?"

"Like what Ingrid?" Martha replied.

"Like the Paris fashion of course!"

"Ingrid you are so shallow," Petra blurted out. "Why on earth did you come on this trip? You could have stayed in your own country and shopped then we wouldn't have to put up with your whining and complaining all the time!"

"Well you don't have to be so rude Petra, and for your information, my parents made me come on this trip, it wasn't by choice I can assure you."

Petra turned and walked away.

"Ingrid, you promised you would try," snapped Gabriella.

"I'm sorry Gabriella, I have tried, I just do not like museums, and I don't know why my parents thought this would do me any good!"

"Are you not enjoying any of this adventure?"

"I wouldn't call it an adventure Gabriella more like torture!" laughed Ingrid.

"Be serious, Ingrid. Your parents are only doing what they think is best for you."

"What, by packing me off somewhere I don't want to be, like they normally do. Let me tell you something Gabriella, my parents are not doing this for my well-being, they are doing what's right for them so they don't have to bother spending time with me. Their work and friends are more important than their own child, so please don't tell me they are doing what's best for me. I am the way that I am because that's how they have made me."

"I'm sorry Ingrid, I didn't realise you were so unhappy I just thought you were being difficult, a spoilt madam."

"That's what everyone thinks of me Gabriella, even my own parents, it makes it easier for them that way."

Gabriella went to hug Ingrid but Ingrid pulled away and went and sat on the coach.

"What's wrong with the drama queen now?" mocked Petra.

"Give her a break Petra, I think I have just seen who the real Ingrid is."

The pyramid style entrance to the museum was very impressive, as was the inside. Once inside, they had the option of an audio headset, which gave them guided information as they went to certain exhibits. Most of the group went for the headset, only a few didn't and Ingrid was one of them. They all went off in different directions after being instructed by Mark to meet back outside the entrance at three o'clock.

The narrator on the audio began the tour.
"The Louvre museum is one of the largest historic monuments in Paris. There are nearly thirty-five thousand objects from prehistory to the twenty first century exhibited here. The Louvre was originally built as a fortress in 1190. If you go into the basement of the museum you can see the original walls. In the sixteenth century it was turned into a renaissance style palace which was the home of King Louis XIV until he moved to Versailles.

At this museum there are many statues. Alexander III of
Macedon better known as Alexander the great, was born in
Pella, the ancient capital of Macedonia in 356BC. His
parents were King Philip II and Queen Olympias.
Alexander was educated by the famous philosopher
Aristotle. At the age of eighteen, Alexander became
cavalry commander, King at twenty, conqueror of the
Persian Empire at twenty-six, and explorer of the Indian
frontier at thirty. He inspired other conquerors such as
Napoleon Bonaparte. Alexander won many a war but died
at the age of thirty-two in Babylon, Persia.

Next, Zeus, the Greek god of the sky who controlled
thunder and lightning. He was easily angered and would
hurl lightning bolts and cause violent storms. His brother,
Poseidon, was the god of the sea and his other brother,
Hades, ruled the underworld.

We have many famous paintings at the Louvre including,
'Adoration of the Shepherds' by Luca Giordano,
'Alexander in Babylon' by Charles Le Brun, and 'A Table
of Deserts' by Jan Davidsz De Heem. But the most famous
of all is Leonardo Da Vinci's 'Mona Lisa'. Over five
hundred years old, it is the greatest and most valuable
painting of all time. In 1911, the painting was stolen but
was recovered in 1913. As a result, the Mona Lisa is now
covered in a bullet proof glass."

As Gabriella continued around the museum she spotted
Ingrid looking very lonely and sad.

"Hi" said Gabriella.

"Hi," replied Ingrid in a soft voice.

"Ingrid I'm sorry, I had no right to judge you without knowing the facts, can you forgive me?"

"Of course I can," smiled Ingrid. "I've lived with it all my life Gabriella, it's just the way it is"

"But it shouldn't be. Your parents are the ones that are meant to take care of you, be there for you."

"Gabriella, really it's okay, can we not talk about it anymore? Let's go find the others and get out of here!"

They looked at each other and laughed.

"Are we all here?" asked Thomas. "It will take us about twenty minutes to walk to Notre Dame so try and stay together."

"What a magnificent building," Petra stated as they approached the cathedral. "It's huge, look at all that beautiful detail."

"So here we are at Notre Dame Cathedral, 'Notre Dame' meaning 'our lady'" shouted Mark amongst the heavy volume of visitors. "It is the largest religious building in the world. Building started in 1163, and by 1345 the Cathedral was opened. It is almost four hundred feet long, one hundred forty feet wide and two hundred feet high. If you are feeling energetic you can climb the three hundred and eighty-seven steps which will take you to the top of the towers. During its construction, many different architects and designers introduced new elements to the Cathedral. As you can see there are many statues on the walls including Quasimodo, the hunchback of Notre Dame. The world's most famous book that was set mostly in the Cathedral written by Victor Hugo, which was then later made into the film. Gargoyles and chimeras were also added to serve as decorative waterspouts.

There are three gates, each one tells its own story. Above the main gate you can see an angel and devil with a scale in between which symbolises all the good deeds and bad deeds that people have done in their lives. The gate to your right is known as the portal of Saint Ann, the Virgin Mary's mother, and displays the story of her marriage to Mary's father, Joachim, the marriage of Mary and Joseph and Christ's arrival on earth. The left gate is known as the portal of the virgin. There are three prophets, Old Testament kings and Mary on her death bed, surrounded by Jesus and the twelve apostles. There are also two angels lifting up Mary's shroud, taking her to heaven and being blessed by Jesus, and crowned as Mary of heaven.

The Cathedral has the world's largest organs and several huge bells. In the south tower they have named the bell 'Emmanuel', it weighs thirteen tons and is only rung in major holidays or events, the other bells will ring every hour to indicate the time.

Now you know some of the history, we will make our way inside, take your time to look around this amazing Cathedral then we will all meet back at the main gate in an hour and half."

"What an amazing place," stated Martha. "Look how high those ceilings go, it is massive in here."

"Truly amazing," replied Petra. "Those stain glass windows are just beautiful."

The girls went their own way, taking in the stunning details of the Cathedral. The paintings and sculptures were

150

exquisite. After about an hour, the sound of the bells rang and then a booming sound from the organ echoed around the cathedral as a choir began to sing.

Gabriella saw that Ingrid was sitting at the front of the cathedral's altar and went to join her.

"Do you mind if I sit with you?" Gabriella asked.

"As long as you don't start asking questions," smiled Ingrid.

Gabriella and Ingrid sat in silence listening to the beautiful sounds of the choir, feeling peaceful and relaxed. Every now and then Gabriella would glance over at Ingrid, she noticed there seem to be a softness in Ingrid's face that she had not seen before. Gabriella prayed for Ingrid, that things would be resolved between her and her parents so that she could be her natural self and not have to pretend to be this spoilt drama queen that everyone saw her as, but to be the lovely beautiful soul that she really was.

As Gabriella opened her eyes and turned to Ingrid, she noticed a beautiful butterfly sitting on Ingrid's shoulder. Where on earth had that come from, Gabriella thought, there's no way a butterfly would be in the Cathedral, there aren't even any outside. She then noticed Ingrid was crying, tears were trickling down her face and she was smiling. As Ingrid opened her eyes, the butterfly flew away.

"Are you okay Ingrid?" enquired Gabriella.

"Yes I'm fine," Ingrid sniffed as she wiped the tears from her face.

Gabriella thought it best not to say anything, but to let Ingrid be in the peaceful place she was in. They both got up and lit a candle, something out of the ordinary for Ingrid.

Martha and Petra caught up with Gabriella and Ingrid. Gabriella looked at Petra as if to say 'don't say a word', as it was obvious that Ingrid had been crying.

"This is a beautiful church," Ingrid commented.

"It's a Cathedral actually," replied Petra sarcastically.

Here we go, thought Gabriella, but surprisingly Ingrid looked at Petra smiled, and laughed. Petra and Martha looked at Gabriella as if to say, 'what? no sarcastic remark back?' From that point Gabriella knew that this was going to be a turning point for Ingrid, and that the butterfly was a sign of new beginnings for her. As they went to meet the rest of the group, Gabriella caught Ingrid looking up to the ceiling with the smile still on her face, saying 'thank you'. Gabriella smiled and also gave thanks.

When they had reached the hostel, Clare gave them their schedule for the rest of the time in Paris. Only three more visits then the rest of the time was their own. This seemed like a good opportunity for Gabriella to call her parents, Macario and her brother Michael whilst the others went back to their rooms.

After her conversation with her parents and reassuring them that everything was okay she called Macario.

"Gabriella I am so looking forward to seeing you. I am flying into Paris tomorrow, I have a few meetings and restaurants to visit over the next couple of days then I am free, what is your schedule?"

"We have three more places to see and that's it. I want to spend a day with my brother Michael, you know the one I told you about who's a chef, then I'm all yours."

"I will call you when I arrive then we can sort out when and where to meet."

"I look forward to it, have a safe journey."

Gabriella then called Michael.

"Michael it's me."

"Gabby I take it you're here in Paris now?"

"Yes, we arrived yesterday, we went to the Louvre museum and Notre Dame Cathedral today."

"That's great, when am I going to see you then so I can book the day off at the restaurant?" Michael asked.

"How about Thursday?"

"That's sounds good, text me where you are staying and I will come and meet you there."

"I can't wait to see you Michael, I have so much to tell you."

"I can't wait either little sis, I'll see you then."

***

The next morning was another early start, they were going to visit the Normandy D-Day and battlefields. The coach was ready and waiting for everyone to board.

"I think this is going to be another one of those emotional visits," said Petra. "Hankies at the ready!"

It was a long journey; they drove through the beautiful Normandy countryside, arriving at Omaha beach where they were greeted by their American guide, Matthew.

"Good morning everyone, welcome to Omaha beach. You may find your visit here a bit overwhelming, but it tells the story of how brave the soldiers were and the trauma they went through in 1944. As we walk over to the museum, you can see outside a landing craft and a Sherman tank that was used. As we go inside you can see there are many historic pieces from the battlefields that were either salvaged or purchased: vehicles, a reconnaissance plane, artillery, posters, signs and lots more. It took many thousands of hours to restore the vehicles in the museum by a team of dedicated skilled specialists. Everything here has information about it, I am going to let you walk around by yourselves, if there are any questions please ask. We will meet in half an hour then walk down to the beach."

They wandered around the museum taking photos and some were sketching the planes and tanks. Matthew then took them down to the beach.

"Ok. June sixth 1944, allied troops invade German-occupied France, it was originally set for June fifth but was postponed due to bad weather. The first wave of attack began with paratroopers; they would jump at night in pitch dark landing behind enemy lines to destroy key targets. Thousands of dummies were dropped in order to draw fire and confuse the enemy.

An artificial harbour was brought from England and put in place to form a breakwater, to facilitate the discharging of vessels bringing war material. Remains of the harbour can still be seen at low tide.

Fifteen thousand aircrafts and seven thousand ships provided coordinate aerial assaults on the beaches and one hundred and fifty thousand ground troops jammed onto hundreds of landing crafts. The landings were made on five beaches. Omaha and Utah is where the American troops landed, Gold and Sword were where the British landed, and Juno, the Canadians. Before the doors were opened, the soldiers could hear the machine guns firing and bullets ricocheting off the landing crafts. As soon as the doors opened, many of the soldiers were instantly shot and killed."

"Oh my word" whispered Martha. "Those poor men didn't stand a chance."

"For those that were lucky enough to get off the boats, their nightmare was just beginning," continued Matthew. "Washed down in wet heavy gear and with bravery and determination, the troops made their way onto the beaches. The Sherman tanks that were released from the landing crafts were much further away from the beach than they realised. Soon after leaving the landing crafts, the tanks were filled with water and began to sink. Nothing could be done to help them, which meant the troops on the beach that expected armoured cover did not get it, resulting in more of them being killed.

At some of the beaches, the allied soldiers met very little resistance, but for Omaha beach, it was like hell on earth. The only way to escape off the beach was to climb the cliffs. Small naval crafts got as close as they could and attacked the German gun emplacements, and by nightfall the Americans had gained a hold on the beach and its immediate hinterland.

At the end of the day, thirty-four thousand American troops landed on this beach, two thousand four hundred of them were casualties. By late August 1944, all of northern France had been liberated.

Looking at this beautiful, quiet and peaceful beach, it's hard to imagine the devastation that took place here. The thousands of troops, landing crafts and ships that covered the beach and seas is something that will never be forgotten.

Before we head up to the memorial cemetery, I will give you some time to just reflect on what happened in those few months in 1944 and to have a little stroll on the beach."

"How brave, they must have been terrified," added Petra. "Imagine living with that nightmare, especially for those that survived."

"I know, it's so sad," replied Gabriella. "It's like you can feel the souls of those that lost their lives."

"If you are all ready, we will head off to the cemetery," Matthew announced.

They made their way up to the cliff top where the cemetery, Colleville-Sur-Mer, was situated.

"This is the resting place of all the brave soldiers whose lives were taken here in Normandy," explained Matthew. "Here in the open arch is the bronze statue, 'The Spirit of American Youth Rising from the Waves', it represents the youth that lost their lives. The average age of the soldiers buried at the cemetery is twenty-two, twenty-three years old. Just beyond the memorial is a semi-circle garden, the garden of the missing, where one thousand five hundred and fifty-seven names are inscribed on the walls of those that were never found."

They all went to the garden to pay their respects to those missing soldiers before going to the plot where the graves lay.

"Look at all these names," said Martha. "So many young lives, they are the same age as us, it just doesn't seem right."

"If we go past the ornamental lake, we take the path that leads us to the grave plots," Matthew informed everyone.

As they approached the graves, Gabriella, Martha, Ingrid and Petra stood there in silence, just as many of the others did. All you could see was a carpet of white crosses and the Star of David for the Jewish soldiers.

"Wow look at all those crosses," gasped Ingrid. "So many lives lost, why we have to have wars and devastation in the world is beyond me. Why can't we all just live in peace and harmony with each other?"

Petra and Martha looked at Gabriella with their mouths open, not quite believing what they just heard. But

Gabriella knew, that whatever happened to Ingrid at Notre Dame had touched her heart.

"There are nine thousand three hundred and eighty-six graves here in the American cemetery," Matthew said quietly. "Each grave faces west towards America. Three hundred and seven of these graves contain the remains of unknown soldiers. As a sign of respect, I ask you all please that we have a minute's silence."

As they stood there in silence Ingrid reached out her hand to Petra, Petra looked at Ingrid with a smile on her face and held her hand in return. After the minute silence, Matthew informed the group that they could go and look at the graves but not to take any photos.

Some of the graves had the soldier's dog tags hanging over them, others had fresh flowers.

"Why are there small stones at the side of the Jewish graves?" enquired Gabriella.

"That is a Jewish custom left by visitors," replied Matthew.

"I know I'm not Jewish," said Ingrid, "but would it be ok if I left a small stone?"

"I'm sure that would be fine."

"That's a lovely gesture Ingrid," smiled Martha. "I think we should all do it."

When they were ready, Matthew walked them back to their coach and thanked them all for coming and for showing respect at the grave plots.

It was a long journey back. They had a packed lunch earlier in the day but was feeling quite hungry, so they stopped off on the way for something to eat before heading back to the hostel.

Tired and emotionally worn out, the girls decided to get an early night, but before they did, Ingrid pulled Gabriella to one side.

"Gabriella I want to thank you."

"Thank me, for what Ingrid?"

"For being my friend and believing in me. Most people get fed up with the way I am and I don't blame them, but you are different, for the first time someone has actually sat and listened to me, made time for me, and that means a lot."

"You don't have to thank me Ingrid, you just needed time to get to know you, and I think that you have."

"What do you mean?"

"I saw something change in you when we went to Notre Dame. I don't know what you saw or heard, if anything, but I do know that the Holy Spirit touched your heart."

"Is that what it was?" Ingrid replied. "I can't explain it to you, but all of a sudden I felt all this forgiveness, for my parents, for those who I thought were my friends, but mostly forgiveness for myself. I knew I had to forgive myself before forgiving them, does that make any sense?"

"Yes it actually does, Ingrid. You know, I think you need to be thanking your parents, if they hadn't insisted on you coming on this journey this may have never happened!"

"I guess you're right. I also need to apologise to Martha and Petra for my behaviour, especially to Petra!"

"You can do all of that tomorrow, let's go to bed it's been a long day."

16

"Bonjour everyone," beamed a happy Ingrid. "What a beautiful day it is, I am just going for a stroll before breakfast, I'll meet you there."

Martha and Petra turned to Gabriella.

"Has Ingrid had a bump on the head? She seems to have changed, she actually held my hand yesterday when we were at the memorial, what was that all about?" laughed Petra.

"Let's just say Ingrid has looked at herself and her life in a different way," Gabriella replied.

"Surely someone who is that spoilt and annoying can't possibly change that much in a short space of time, has she suddenly seen the light!?" mocked Petra.

"You could say that," smiled Gabriella.

"Okay, we will see how long it lasts!" Petra teased as she went to have a shower.

Martha looked at Gabriella.

"It's you."

"I know it's me," laughed Gabriella. "Are you ok Martha?"

"It's you, when we went to that Cathedral in Malta, something happened to me do you remember, when I started crying and couldn't explain why? You told me that the Holy Spirit had touched my heart."

"Yes I remember," replied Gabriella. "But what's that got to do with me?"

"Now that I think about it, Ingrid has only changed since we were at Notre Dame and you were with her then. It may be coincidental but there's something special about you Gabriella Rossini, you seem to help people in a spiritual way when they most need it. Look at me, I would have never realised something was missing in my life, but since that day it has made me think about things in a different way and that's because of you. It's not just the Holy Spirit that touches hearts Gabriella!"

"Don't be daft Martha, I was just pointing out to you and Ingrid that the Holy Spirit comes to us when we least expect it."

"So that's what you told Ingrid, that the Holy Spirit had touched her heart?"

"Well yes I guess so, but Martha I'm Catholic and I go to church, so I do know about the Holy Spirit."

"No Gabriella, there's more to it than that. I don't think you have even seen it yourself yet!"

Petra came back from the shower, dressed and ready to go to breakfast.

At breakfast, Gabriella couldn't stop thinking about what Martha had said. She thought back to all the strange things that had happened since she began this journey. She remembered what Macario told her, that there was no such thing as coincident, everything happens for a reason. Is there really something in what Martha had said?

"Ok folks, today we are going to the Arc de Triomphe," announced Susan, "then we shall take a walk down one of the most famous avenues in the world and the top Paris shopping district, Champs Elysees. We will be taking the Metro to Charles de Gaulle. So if we are all ready, let's go."

"That will be right up Ingrid's street," mocked Petra. "Talking of, where is Ingrid?"

"Wait for me!" shouted Ingrid. "Sorry I didn't realise what time it was."

Once they arrived at Charles de Gaulle they took the exit at Etoile. There was no mistake of where they were, the Arc de Triomphe was in front of you, you could not miss it. When they got to the Arc de Triomphe, Mark told them of some of its history.

"As you can see this is a remarkable monument. It was commissioned by Napoleon and designed in 1806 to honour those who fought for France, and to celebrate the victory of Napoleon, but it was never actually completed until 1836. The arc stands at one hundred and sixty-four feet high, one hundred and forty eight feet wide and seventy two feet deep. This huge arc has two full towers, one each side. You can see sculptured friezes of soldiers depicted upon the masonry. If you look up in the attic you can see thirty shields which are engraved with the names of major revolutionary and Napoleonic military victories.

Along the inside of the walls are the engraved names of five hundred and fifty-eight generals, underlined are the names of those that died in battle.

The Arc de Triomphe is also home to the tomb of the unknown soldiers that gave their lives, and were never identified from World War I and World War II. An eternal flame burns in memory of those that died. Over the years, many political figures have paid their respect at the tomb.

Any questions so far? Then I will continue.

The views from the top are breath-taking, you can get a great view of the Eiffel Tower. It is certainly one of the most marvellous pieces of architecture and also the second largest triumphal arcs.

The Arc de Triomphe has become a focal point for many events. One of the main events that it is known for, from all over the world, is the famous cycle race, The Tour de France. This plays an important part to the participants because as soon as they see the Arc, they know that the race is almost finished.

I hope I have given you enough information about this wonderful monument, if you have any questions I will try and answer them for you. Take your time and have a closer look at the beautiful sculptures and when you're ready, we will walk down to Champs Elysees."

"This is beautiful," announced Ingrid. "The work that has gone into it is just perfect."

"Since when have you been into architecture?" Petra voiced sarcastically.

"Since now I guess," replied Ingrid as she carried on walking around the arc.

"No, she's having us on," remarked Petra. "Ingrid is as interested in monuments as much as I am in spending the day walking around designer clothes shops!"

Gabriella and Martha looked at each other and laughed.

"If you have all finished, we will head off to the Champs Elysees. I know this won't be to every ones liking," explained Mark, "so we will only spend half an hour there as it is extremely expensive! For those of you who wish to spend more time wandering around the shops, remember, after today you have your own time to explore before we leave Paris."

As they reached the Champs Elysees you can just see a large show room of famous brand names, Cartier, Swarovski, Dior, Louis Vuitton, Zara. Too many to mention. They walked past some of the cafes and restaurants, and Petra looked at the menus.

"Have you seen the prices of the food and drink? It's ridiculous!" Petra shrieked. "And the clothes, it's daylight robbery!"

"Careful Petra you're beginning to sound like Ingrid, complaining about everything!" laughed Gabriella.

"Please, don't say that, I think I've been around here too long, no offence Ingrid."

"None taken," she replied, "I think it's rather funny."

After their short tour of the Champs Elysees they headed back to the Metro to reach the hostel.

"Can I have your attention," yelled Thomas. "As you know this is our last time out as a group, so we thought you would enjoy seeing a show. We have booked to go to the famous Moulin Rouge to have dinner and watch the cabaret show. So enjoy the rest of your afternoon, our coach will be picking us up at 6pm."

The girls sat in their room discussing what they would be doing with their remaining days in Paris.

"Martha, what will you be doing?" asked Ingrid.

"I'm not sure yet, I think I will just go wherever the wind takes me."

"But there is no wind Martha, it's lovely and sunny," Ingrid replied.

"Oh Ingrid," laughed Martha, "it's just a saying! I mean I will do whatever inspires me at the time."

"How about you, Petra?"

"I quite fancy a few art galleries and maybe finding a few gifts to take back home."

"Gabriella?"

"Well I need to catch up filling in my journal, I'm meeting up with my brother, and Macario is coming for a few days."

"Really, I forgot all about him," said Petra. "Wow, talk about a holiday romance!"

"And what about you Ingrid?" asked Gabriella, changing the subject pretty quickly.

"No doubt hitting the designer shops!" interrupted Petra.

"Actually Petra, I was going to ask you if I could tag along to one of your art galleries, if that's okay?"

Petra stood there, stunned, taken aback and feeling slightly embarrassed.

"Sure," Petra stuttered, "as long as you don't complain about everything?"

"Great, now that we have got that sorted out, let's get ready for a night at the Moulin Rouge! It will take us the rest of the afternoon," laughed Martha.

***

On the way to the Moulin Rouge, everyone was chatting excitedly.

"Did you know that the Moulin Rouge opened in 1889, the same time as the Eiffel Tower opened," Petra informed the girls. "Edith Piaf first found fame on the stage of the Moulin Rouge."

"Edith who?" asked Ingrid.

"Edith Piaf, she was a famous cabaret singer, songwriter and actress, one of France's greatest stars. Many renowned artists have performed at the Moulin Rouge on gala nights.

Ginger Rogers, Ella Fitzgerald, Ray Charles, even Elton John."

"Well I have only heard of one of those, and that's Elton John!" replied Ingrid.

"The theatre is situated in the middle of the red light district at Montmartre," said Petra. "Think we better stick together!" Petra laughed nervously. "Oh look we're here."

The Moulin Rouge and the boulevards were lit up with bright lights. Everyone got off the coach and walked down to the theatre.

"Ladies and gents, there will be five to a table," Mark told everyone. "Myself, Thomas, Clare and Susan will sit at each table, to make sure you're behaving!" he laughed.

Susan sat with Gabriella, Ingrid, Martha and Petra. Once seated, they ordered their meals and had a few glasses of wine, except Ingrid.

"Not drinking Ingrid?" Martha asked.

"No, I'm quite happy thank you."

"Go on," encouraged Petra, "it's our very last night out together."

"Petra, I can have just as much of a good time without drinking."

"Are you sure we have the right Ingrid with us?" joked Petra.

After the meal had finished and a few more glasses of wine were had, the show began. The lights went dim, the music began to play, and the dancers came on. Sixty Doriss girls came out in the most beautiful costumes, followed by the twenty Doriss boys. The music and singing was all in French, but you could still enjoy the entertainment and understand what was happening without understanding the lyrics.

"This is a marvellous show," yelled Martha over the loud music, "their costumes are stunning."

No one could really hear what Martha was saying. Best to just enjoy the show then speak in the interval. There were so many different acts: Russian dancing, acrobats and jugglers. It was a very entertaining show.

"Wow, it's very loud but most enjoyable," smiled Ingrid in the interval. "The ladies don't wear much clothing do they?"

"That's what the Moulin Rouge is all about Ingrid!" laughed Petra. "Did you know that Toulouse - Lautrec was a regular here at the theatre, this is where he found inspiration for his sketches of singers and dancers."

"That's what I like about you Petra, you're so knowledgeable about things."

"Thanks Ingrid, I like you too really, but don't tell anyone!"

The lights went dim again and the show continued. The second half was packed full of dance, song and costume changes, even a circus act. Then the stage cleared and a giant tank rose up, filled with water and lots of live snakes, big ones and small ones, there were also boa constrictors!

"What on earth is going to happen with them?" asked an inquisitive Martha.

A woman appeared wearing only a nude coloured thong, dived into the middle of the water and swam with the snakes winding them around her body.

"Is that woman mad!?" Ingrid yelled. "There are boa constrictors in there, they could squeeze her to death."

"I'm sure she is aware of the dangers Ingrid; she knows what she's doing," reassured Gabriella.

"I hope you're right Gabriella, otherwise this could turn out very bad!"

The evening was drawing to an end, but not before the finale, the famous Cancan dance. The ladies wore blue, red and white ruffled petticoats, the music was loud, the dance was fast with legs kicking everywhere, and the audience were on their feet with excitement, humming the tune of the dance. The final kick and split and the show was over. The audience cheered and clapped, some even shouted 'viva la France! Long live France.'

"That was one of the best shows I have ever seen," yelled a beaming Ingrid.

"You don't have to shout Ingrid, we're outside now," laughed Martha.

The girls were all chatting with excitement on the coach journey back to the hostel.

"Listen up guys!" announced Thomas. "It has been a great evening and a great few months spent with you all. There are only three full days left before we head back home, so enjoy your time here and we will meet up at six thirty in the morning on our last day. Try and be on time as we need to get to the airport so that you can all catch your individual flights back. Have a good night's sleep."

Gabriella, Martha, Petra and Ingrid were still excited from the night's entertainment, they stayed up talking for a while before going off to sleep.

***

Gabriella woke up before the others so she started to fill in her journal.

I can't believe that my adventure is almost over. I have seen the most amazing places and met some beautiful people. It has been everything that I had dreamed of as a child, and more. There have been some strange things that have happened to me that I am still trying to understand, but I know I will be leaving here with the most wonderful memories.

I can't wait to see Michael today, we have so much to catch up with and of course seeing Macario again. I can already feel the butterflies in my tummy! I know we have only just met but, I don't know, there is something so special about him. This is going to sound so silly and probably childish, but I honestly feel we are going to have an amazing relationship! I guess time will tell. I can hear Petra, Ingrid and Martha starting to wake up now. I will miss them, and they will be my friends for life.

"Morning ladies, did you sleep well?" asked Gabriella.

"How long have you been up?" replied Ingrid.

"A few hours. I've written in my journal and now off for breakfast, then meeting my brother. I hope you all have a lovely day; I'll see you sometime this evening."

"You have a good day too Gabriella."

After breakfast Gabriella waited excitedly outside the hostel for her brother Michael.

"Gabby."

Gabriella turned round and could see Michael coming towards her. She ran up to him and they gave each other the biggest hug.

"Michael, it's so good to see you, I have missed you so much."

"Me too Gabby. You are looking great, I think you have put a few pounds on, sis," he said playfully, poking her tummy.

"Thanks, it's all this continental cuisine! So where are you taking me?"

"I thought we would go on a cruise boat on the Seine River."

"Sounds great."

"Good. Let's go then."

It was a beautiful sunny day. They boarded a big double decker open boat and gentle sailed off down the Seine.

"Tell me all about your exciting life here in Paris, Michael?"

"Where do I start? As you can see, it's a beautiful country, I have met so many interesting people, the way of life here is so relaxed and of course I love my work. I live in a small studio apartment near the Eiffel Tower, what more could I ask for?"

"Do you think you will go back to Italy?"

"To be totally honest Gabby, no, my life is here now, I will work hard so I can achieve my dream of owning my own restaurant."

"You know that mama and papa are not going to be happy about that, their dream is for you to open your own restaurant in Italy. I don't think I want to be around when you tell them!"

"But that's just it Gabby, it's their dream not mine, they will have to respect what I want. Anyway, enough of me, tell me about your travels. Has it been everything that you dreamed of?"

"Oh yes Michael, it really has, I have seen the most wonderful places, experienced different types of food and cultures and learnt a lot of history, and met some lovely people. My roommates on this entire journey have been amazing, we have had our moments but they are great! I will definitely be staying in touch with them once I return to Italy. I have also met a boy, his name is Macario and we met in Madeira."

Gabriella continued to tell Michael the whole story of how they met, and about the strange things that had happened, and how much she had fallen for Macario. She also told him that Macario felt the same about her.

"Wow Gabby, that's some adventure you've been on! This Macario, when are you planning on seeing him again?"

"Well actually, he is flying into Paris tomorrow on business for a few days. I would love you to meet him Michael, I think you would get on really well as you are both in the same line of business."

"I'll tell you what, bring him to the restaurant tomorrow, it will be nice to see who this boy is that has captured my little sister's heart! For now, let's enjoy the time we have together."

They continued on their trip down the Seine River passing the Concorde, Louvre Museum, Hotel de Ville, Notre Dame and then finally getting off at the Eiffel Tower.

"I would suggest we go up the Eiffel Tower, the views from there are amazing, but I think I will leave that one for you and the boyfriend to explore!" teased Michael. "Let's go up to my apartment and I'll cook lunch."

Once in Michael's apartment, Gabriella commented on how small it was.

"Gabby, it's a studio apartment, they aren't meant to be big! I manage quite well actually, It's only me that lives here so I don't need much space. Now what can I rustle up for you?"

"Do you know what I would like, a big bowl of pasta and meat balls," Gabriella replied.

"Missing home by any chance?" Michael enquired.

"No not really, but I do miss mamas meatballs," laughed Gabriella.

Gabriella and Michael spent a lovely day together catching up with everything, but it was getting late, and time for Gabriella to go back to the hostel. On their way back they walked down the canal Saint-Martin. It was where groups of people would gather around, generally with a guitar or some kind of musical instrument. They stayed for a while enjoying the company and music before continuing back.

"I've had a wonderful day Michael. Thank you."

"It's been great spending time with you, sis, and hearing all of your exciting news, come by the restaurant tomorrow with Macario and see where I work my magic!"

Gabriella and Michael laughed as they gave each other a big hug. She waved Michael off then went into the hostel and up to her room. Petra, Martha and Ingrid were having a game of cards when Gabriella came in.

"Hi Gabriella, how was your day with Michael?" asked Ingrid.

"I had a wonderful day thank you, we went on a boat cruise on the Seine, then Michael took me to his apartment and cooked lunch. We had a lot to catch up with, I don't know where the time went. Then on the way home we went by this canal where people gathered around and played musical instruments, it was great. What did you all do?"

"Well, Ingrid and I went to the Musee Picasso art gallery," said Petra. "The man was a genius. Even Ingrid enjoyed it."

"That's right, I certainly did, I never knew that paintings could tell a story if you really look at them. It has made me look at art in a completely different way."

"I'm glad you enjoyed it," smiled Gabriella.

"And where did the wind take you Martha?"

"I went to the oldest bridge in Paris, Pont Neuf. It is built over the River Seine; you must have gone under it on your boat cruise Gabriella? It has some interesting statues on it like the equestrian of Henri IV wearing his armour and holding a sceptre bearing the royal emblem. Fleur De Lys which means Lily flower. It was a lovely walk."

Just then Gabriella's phone rang.

"Excuse me whilst I answer this."

"Gabriella, it's me Macario,"

"Macario where are you?" Gabriella asked excitedly.

"I've just arrived in Paris, I'm at the hotel. I have to go and look at one of the restaurants my father wants to buy in the morning for a few hours, then I'm free for the rest of the day, can you meet me at the Eiffel Tower, say eleven o'clock?"

"Of course I will Macario, I'm so looking forward to seeing you."

"Me too Gabriella, sleep well and I'll see you tomorrow."

As Gabriella turned around, all eyes were on her, she had totally forgotten the girls were there.

"No guesses to who that was then!" laughed Petra. "Gabriella, you're going red."

"Leave her alone Petra," said Ingrid giving her a nudge.

"I didn't mean anything Gabriella; I think it's lovely."

"Well I think it's time for bed!" Martha tried to save Gabriella from any more of Petra's comments.

Gabriella lay there, excited, picturing Macario's handsome face and dark hair. She gave her teddy bear a hug, the one Gabriella's friends had given her when she left Italy, imagining it was Macario. Then she slowly drifted off to sleep.

17

It was a beautiful sunny morning and the girls all woke around the same time.

"Morning," yawned Ingrid. "What a lovely day it is."

"It's glorious!" Gabriella exclaimed as she jumped out of bed. "I'm just going for a shower."

"She looks so happy," observed Petra. "I hope he really likes Gabriella as much as she likes him?"

Gabriella had her shower, got dressed and went for breakfast, not that she felt like eating much as she felt quite nervous about seeing Macario again. Excitedly she left the hostel and made her way to the Metro. As she reached the Eiffel Tower, her tummy was jumping all over the place, and then she saw him. Gabriella took a deep breath and made her way over to Macario.

"Hi."

Macario turned around, he gazed deeply into Gabriella's eyes.

"Gabriella, you look beautiful," he said as they gently embraced. "At last, I've been counting the days until I could see you again."

"Me too," said Gabriella nervously. "How did your meeting go at the restaurant?"

"Really well, I think it's the right restaurant to buy. It has an excellent chef and it's in a good location but I need to run it by my father first. How have you been? Let's go and have a coffee and you can tell me all of your news."

They found a lovely café close by. Gabriella told Macario all of the wonderful places she had travelled to.

"Sounds like you have had an adventure. What has been your best country?"

"Madeira of course!" Gabriella blushed. "It's been a fabulous experience, it's a shame it has to end."

"It's not ended yet." Macario took Gabriella's hand. "Let's finish our coffee then go up to the Eiffel Tower, have you been up there?"

"No, my brother was going to take me but he suggested I saw it with you. Which reminds me, he has invited us to the restaurant he works at for dinner this evening."

"Sounds great, I'm looking forward to meeting this wonderful chef you've told me about."

As they reached the Eiffel Tower, Macario and Gabriella thought it would be fun to walk up to the second floor of the tower, all seven hundred and four steps.

"We must be mad!" spluttered a breathless Gabriella. "I can't believe we walked all those steps, I'm exhausted."

"You're right about that," replied Macario. "But look at the view, isn't it just amazing?"

They couldn't find a better spot to take some photos of their view of Paris. After they had got their breath back they took the lift up to the top of the tower.

"Look, a champagne bar. Would Mademoiselle care for a glass of champagne?"

"That would be lovely. Merci Monsieur. You wouldn't want to come up here if you suffered from vertigo! I wonder how high up we are."

They took their champagne and went outside to see the rest of the view.

"To answer your question, we are nine hundred and eighty-six feet high," Macario informed Gabriella. "This is spectacular; you can see everywhere." He drew Gabriella closer to him.

Gabriella had never felt so happy, she felt dizzy, not because of the champagne or how high up they were, but for her feelings for Macario. After an hour of looking at the views and just holding each other, they made their way back to the bottom of the tower. They walked through the park laughing and joking and enjoying being with each other. Before they realised it the sun was going down and night was approaching. They made their way to the restaurant that Michael worked at.

"Gabriella are you sure this is the right restaurant?"

"Yes, I think so, this is where Michael said to come, why?"

"You are not going to believe this, but this is the restaurant that I came to look at this morning."

"Macario, you're kidding me?"

"I'm not, this is possibly going to be our new restaurant and your brother is the excellent chef I was telling you about!"

Gabriella and Macario just stood there, looked at each other, then burst into laughter.

"I guess we had better go in, I can then meet the man himself!"

"Your back so soon Monsieur Rico," the maître d' enquired. "Let me show you to your table, I will bring you the menu."

"I didn't know your last name was Rico," Gabriella remarked. "Macario Rico, it has a nice ring to it."

"Thank you Miss Rossini, I assume you have the same surname as your brother?"

"How do you know our name if you have not met Michael?"

"The maître d' told me all the names of the staff when I came this morning."

The maître d' brought over the menus and some complimentary champagne. "If I could be so bold and recommend the chefs special. For the entrée, Lobster with Pomelo, Papaya, Caviar and yuzu dressing and for the main course, Veal slowly cooked with duck liver, black truffle and truffle sauce?"

"That sounds good. Gabriella, what do you think?"

"Yes, that's fine thank you. Macario don't you think we should let Michael know that we are here?"

"We will, let's eat first."

After they had finished their meal, Macario asked to see the chef.

"Macario, what are you doing?"

"Gabriella, why didn't you let me know you were here," announced Michael. "I have to see a customer then I'll be back."

"Michael this is Macario, he's the customer that wanted to see you."

"Michael, it's nice to meet you." He shook his hand. "I just wanted to tell you that your food was exquisite, you should think about opening your own restaurant."

"I'm sorry I don't understand? Gabby has told me all about you and thank you for the compliment, but I'm a bit confused." He looked at Gabriella.

"Can you meet us after your shift, I would like to talk to you?"

"Sure, I finish at eleven o'clock."

Gabriella looked at Michael and shrugged her shoulders as if to say that she had no clue what was going on.

"Are you going to tell me what you're playing at?" demanded Gabriella, now feeling a bit cross.

"Please don't be angry with me Gabriella, let's go for a walk and I'll explain. When I went to look at the restaurant this morning, I was almost sure that my father would buy it, as I said before, it's in a good location, it has a good clientele and I heard that it had an excellent chef! Then this evening I meet that excellent chef and tasted his food, which convinced me one hundred per cent that when I report back to my father, he will definitely buy it."

"So why do you want to see Michael?"

"Can I explain when we see Michael? It will all make sense then, actually it all seems a bit crazy and mad but remember everything happens for a reason!"

***

Michael had finished for the evening and went to meet Macario and Gabriella at a local bar. Gabriella gave Michael a big hug and Macario thanked him for coming.

"I was very impressed by your cooking this evening, I don't know if you knew, but I was there at the restaurant this morning. My father is interested in buying the restaurant, that's our family business, buying restaurants. Gabriella told me that you're a chef but when we got there this evening I had no idea that it was the same place you worked at."

"I still don't understand, and no, I didn't know it was being sold, I hope I still have a job?" Michael looked at Gabriella with a worried look on his face, he had worked so hard to get this job and it was a good restaurant.

"That's what I want to talk to you about. For some time now I have wanted my own project, my own restaurant to start from scratch. My father said to me if I was to find the right building, all the right materials for the restaurant, staff, suppliers he would fund it for me and that I would have total control. I would like it to be a three star Michelin restaurant eventually. I know this is going to sound really crazy but I think you're the right chef to achieve that."

Michael and Gabriella looked at each other stunned.

"But you don't even know me and you've only tasted one meal, how can you decide just by that?"

"I told you it would sound crazy, but I am usually a pretty good judge of character, I always go with my gut instinct and it has never let me down before. You would have full control of the kitchen, the menus, where we get the food from, the hiring of the kitchen staff. I have been looking for the right person to come in with me for some time, and I have not found any one up until now."

"And if I did decide to do this, where would the restaurant be?"

"In my hometown of Madeira."

"Madeira! I don't know, I always imagined myself staying in Paris and owning my own restaurant here."

"You would be your own boss, the building would be mine, but when it comes to the food and the three Michelin stars that I know you will achieve, the recognition will be all yours. Then if you still want to go your own way in the future I won't stand in your way. Michael it's a great opportunity for both of us."

"This is all a bit much to take in, I could not possibly give you an answer now. I'll need some time to think about it."

"Take as long as you like, here are my details." Macario handed Michael a card. "I'm still here until tomorrow evening if you want to ask me any questions."

After a few drinks Michael went back to his apartment, and Macario walked Gabriella back to the hostel.

"Well that was an interesting evening," laughed Gabriella. "Are you sure about this Macario, you know nothing about Michael? Not that there is anything bad about him, he is probably one of the kindest, most hard-working, loving people that I know, but that's because he's my brother and I know him. You've known him for five minutes, and you don't really know me that well either."

"Gabriella I feel as though I have always known you, and I know you feel the same. Look at all the things that have happened since we met, all the signs given to us. It's meant to be, we are meant to be. Remember the lady on the catamaran in Madeira and what she said, about you being a very spiritual person? I truly believe that too, and how you would be doing something special on the island, well you have already. Through you I have met Michael and hopefully he will take me up on my offer... and I also hope that maybe in time, you might consider moving to Madeira as well. There is something special waiting for you there Gabriella, where you will make a difference."

Gabriella looked at Macario in surprise, she was not expecting to hear that, but for some reason it felt right.

Macario looked lovingly into Gabriella's eyes and kissed her. Fireworks exploded in her head and butterflies danced wildly in her tummy. They both looked at each other in some sort of daze.

"I better go in," said a flustered Gabriella, everyone will be asleep now, I didn't realise it was so late. "Will I see you tomorrow?"

"You try stopping me. I will come and pick you up about ten thirty? We can spend the whole day together; my flight leaves at eight o'clock so I need to be at the airport by seven. I only have hand luggage so I don't need to check in any bags."

Macario kissed Gabriella again, watched her go in then left. Gabriella crept quietly into the room where the girls were fast asleep and slipped into bed. What a crazy day that was, she thought to herself. She drifted off to sleep with a lovely smile on her face.

Hours later, Gabriella was woken by a call from her phone, she grabbed it quickly and left the room so she would not wake the girls, it was Michael.

"Michael are you okay? It's only seven o'clock what's wrong?"

"Morning sis, sorry I woke you. I've been awake most of the night thinking about what Macario said. Is he for real?"

"Yes he is Michael, I must say, I was just as surprised as you, I knew nothing about this."

"But he knows nothing about me or my cooking. Sorry to sound suspicious Gabby, but people don't just come along, have one meal then offer you this amazing opportunity! This is my career; one I have worked very hard at. If I'm that good, which I know I am," he laughed, "then why doesn't he just leave me to continue in the restaurant I'm already at, seeing that his family will soon own it, it doesn't make sense Gabby."

"I'll talk to Macario about it when I see him later. I know everything is happening so fast Michael, I haven't known him for long either but there is something about him, all the things that I told you that have happened since I met Macario, even his mother coming from a town not far from us in Italy, so many things just fit into place like a jigsaw puzzle, it's crazy I know, but it just feels right Michael."

"I don't know Gabby, I never thought I would leave Paris I love it here, it's my home."

"Leave it with me Michael, and I will get back to you later."

Gabriella went back to her room where Martha, Ingrid and Petra were now awake.

"Where were you last night, you must have got back late?" enquired Petra.

"Sorry I didn't mean to worry you; it was a very interesting, mad and crazy day!"

Gabriella told them what had happened.

"What?! Gabriella, you have either met the most wonderful man that only exist in dreams, or he is a complete psychopath!" laughed Petra.

"Petra, that's a horrible thing to say," said Ingrid.

"But you don't know, it's not like you have known Macario for very long," Martha added.

"Ladies stop worrying, trust me that I know he is genuine, and yes Petra he is a wonderful man. I best get ready, Macario will be here soon."

Ten thirty on the dot Macario arrived, eagerly waiting for Gabriella.

"Good morning gorgeous did you sleep well?" Macario gave Gabriella a kiss.

"I did until Michael called me early this morning. He's concerned about your offer, he's not sure if your serious. He needs to know that he will still have financial security, somewhere to live. It's a big move for him, Paris is his home now. What he can't understand is why him? If he was that much of a good asset why not just keep him on where he already is?"

"Michael has nothing to worry about Gabriella, I've been in and around this business long enough to know an excellent chef when I see one. Yes, we could keep him on there, but I really believe that he will flourish more in Madeira. Madeira needs more excellent chefs, plus he would have more input right from the start as if it were his own. We would still continue to pay him until things are up and running, he will get twice as much as he is earning now and we will provide accommodation for him."

"When you put it like that, how could he refuse," laughed Gabriella. "It would be a great opportunity for him"

"Now, can we not talk about Michael?" joked Macario. "Let's enjoy the time that we have left! I thought we could take the metro to the Sacre Coeur, is that okay with you?"

"Sounds perfect."

As they reached the Sacre Coeur, situated on Montmarte Hill, they stood and looked at all the stairs to climb.

"Shall we take the elevator to the top or be really fit and walk up the ninety steps?" said Macario.

"I'll race you to the top!" Gabriella shrieked as she started to run.

"Wait, that's cheating!" Macario ran after her.

Once at the top they both collapsed on the steps laughing. Macario leant over and gave Gabriella a loving kiss. Once they had got their breath back they made their way into the church, hand in hand.

"It's so beautiful," observed Gabriella. "It's so big, so may pews."

"Did you know that Sacre Coeur is dedicated to the Sacred Heart of Jesus? It was completed in 1912 and opened 1914."

Gabriella laughed.

"Have I said something amusing?" asked a puzzled Macario.

"No, I'm sorry, you sound like Petra who's one of my roommates. Every time we go somewhere she always gives us the information about where we are, it just made me chuckle." Gabriella gave Macario's hand a gentle squeeze.

They continued around the church, admiring the colourful stained glass windows and the most beautiful mosaic on the ceiling of the Apse of Christ, with his arms outstretched with the sacred heart on his white gown, surrounded by the saints who protect France, the Virgin Mary and Saint Michael. The whole church gave the atmosphere of peace and harmony.

"Shall we go up to the bell tower?" Macario asked Gabriella. "Do you think your legs can make it up the three hundred stairs?"

"Of course they will, but will yours?" teased Gabriella.

After having a look in the crypt, they made their way up to the bell tower, stopping several times to rest! It is the second highest view point after the Eiffel Tower. Once they reached the top they were taken aback by the most beautiful view.

"Oh Macario just look how stunning the view is? It was definitely worth that exhausting climb."

They stood there embraced in each other's arms, for which seemed like hours before making their way back down those three hundred stairs!

When they had reached the bottom they could hear the Organ playing, a mass was about to begin. Gabriella and Macario sat at one of the hundreds of pews. They could not understand what was being said as it was all in French, but that didn't really matter, they were happy just sitting and experiencing the peacefulness.

As the service was coming to an end everyone was asked to kneel to receive a blessing. That much they could understand. Gabriella and Macario joined hands and bowed their heads. The mass ended and people started to leave, but Gabriella and Macario stayed and continued to pray. They both looked up at the mosaic they had seen when they first came into the church, with its beautiful colours of blue and gold. It was as if Christ was inviting them into his arms. Then they both felt a gentle breeze go across their face.

"Did you feel that?" Gabriella whispered to Macario.

"Yes. I know churches can feel chilly but I have never felt a breeze like that in one before."

"It's another one of those strange things happening," Gabriella replied.

"I feel it's just more confirmation that we are meant to be together, too many things keep happening. It's showing us to listen, listen to our hearts." explained Macario. "Gabriella all I know is that when I'm with you I am at my happiest, and when I'm apart from you I feel like a part of me is missing. I have never had these feelings for anyone before, I know it's only been a short time and we have only seen each other a few times but do you believe in love at first sight? That's how I feel. I love you Gabriella."

"I love you too, Macario. I wish you didn't have to go back to Madeira so soon."

"I know, but you're going back to Italy tomorrow, so then we can start making plans."

"What sort of plans Macario?"

"For us to always be together."

Macario and Gabriella both looked up to the heavens and gave thanks.

The rest of their day went so quickly and soon it was time for Macario to catch his plane.

"I'm going to miss you Macario, will you call me when you get home?"

"Of course I will. You take care of yourself Gabriella, and have a safe journey back to Italy. Love you."

They held each other for as long as they could and gently kissed before saying their goodbyes.

Gabriella went into the hostel, up to her room and started on her packing for her return journey back to Italy. Martha, Petra and Ingrid were already packing.

"How was your day Gabriella?" enquired Martha.

"It was wonderful thank you Martha, except for saying goodbye to Macario, but we will see each other soon." Gabriella smiled.

When they had all finished packing they went and had a final drink together, reflecting back on their journey.

"We've had some great times together," smiled Martha. "My most memorable time was when we went to the concentration camp in Germany. That is something I shall never forget."

"Mine was when Ingrid thought she was drowning when she put her face in the water when we went snorkelling, that was so funny, miss drama queen!"

"That was not funny Petra, well maybe it was," laughed Ingrid. "My best time was Notre Dame. That was the day that turned my life around, for the better of course! And meeting you guys, you changed my life too and I will never forget you. What about you Gabriella, or do I need to ask!?"

"Of course meeting Macario! But this whole journey has been the best time ever, an experience I will never forget. Every single moment has been educational, exciting, emotional, and hilarious, and one of the happiest times of my life! And as Ingrid said, meeting you guys... it wouldn't have been the same without you. I hope we'll stay friends forever!"

They had a big group hug, finished their drink and headed back to the hostel for the last time. As they got back, Gabriella got a call from Michael.

"Gabby I didn't wake you did I?"

"No Michael, we just got back from our farewell drink, are you okay?"

"Yes, well I think so. I've been thinking about Macario's offer, I must be mad but I'm going to do it. Looks like I'm going to Madeira."

"Michael!" screeched Gabriella. "That's great news, you won't regret it, Macario has reassured me that everything will be fine. You never know, I may be joining you!"

"Gabby, what are you saying? You've only just met him, you can't just pack everything up leave the family and your friends and move to Madeira."

"Why not? You are."

"But this is work, that's different. Mama and papa will go mad."

"Just like they will when they know you're not going back to Italy! Michael please be happy for me; I know it sounds crazy but we love each other."

"Love, Gabby how can you be in love with someone you've only known for five minutes."

"Just like you Michael, it's about having trust and faith. I know it is right Michael, I feel it in my heart. It's not like it's going to happen overnight, you will be there before me, and mama and papa will be fine knowing that you'll be there looking after me."

"I doubt that very much Gabby! But if you are really serious about this then you're right, at least I will be there to look out for you. I'll call Macario and tell him the good news, I just hope we are both doing the right thing! Have a safe journey home, give my love to mama, papa, Anthony and Mario. Good luck when you tell them! Love you."

"Don't worry, everything will be fine, trust me. I'll speak to you soon, love you too."

Gabriella, Martha, Petra and Ingrid all settled down for the night, their last night together, knowing that when they woke up it would be Au Revoir!

***

Morning had arrived, and everyone was up early. They had had breakfast and were waiting in the reception area for the coach to arrive to take them to the airport.

"Can I have your attention please," announced Susan. "Before we leave I would just like to say thank you to you all from us, for being such a great bunch of people on this journey. You have made us laugh... some more than others! We hope you have enjoyed your experience with us and maybe we will see you again for another adventure. The coach has now arrived so if we can start boarding we will be off to the airport."

At the airport it was time for everyone to say their goodbyes. Gabriella, Ingrid, Petra and Martha gathered together in a huddle.

"I am really going to miss you guys," said an emotional Ingrid. "Thank you for putting up with me and my tantrums! I came on this journey very reluctantly as my parents thought it would do me 'good' and do you know what, they were right, for once they actually did the right thing! I came here a spoilt drama queen and I'm going back a completely different person, a more likeable one I hope! And that's down to you guys and the good Lord himself."

"Aww Ingrid that was lovely," Petra gushed, struggling to keep her emotions intact. "I must say you were a real pain in the you know what to start with, and I was probably the one that gave you the most stick about it, so I apologise for that, but you turned out good and am glad we became friends"

The flight departures were being announced.

"That's my plane," Gabriella told the girls. "Well I guess this is it then, I'm going to miss you all, you have my address and phone number, please stay in touch."

With that they gave each other one last hug and went their separate ways. Gabriella felt sad but what a story she had to tell when she got home. Just then Gabriella's phone rang.

"Gabriella, its Macario. Just to let you know I'm home and that I'm missing you already, I've told my parents about you, well I had told my mother about you before I left for Paris and they are looking forward to meeting you. Michael called me with the good news about coming to Madeira, I told my father about him setting up the restaurant with me and he is happy about it."

"That's great Macario, I miss you too, I'm looking forward to meeting your parents, but I must say I'm not looking forward to telling my parents about you, I can hear my mother and father now! Well you know what Italians are like, very protective over their children and especially that I am their only daughter. I thought telling them I was going travelling was bad enough, but this!" laughed Gabriella.

"We will get through it Gabriella; your parents will love me!" joked Macario.

"I know they will, just like I do. Macario I have to go; they are announcing last call for my flight. I'll call you when I'm home, and when I've spoken to my parents."

Gabriella ran to the boarding gate, making it just in time. She found her seat and smiled to herself, thinking of Macario and the whole adventure she had. The plane took off. Gabriella was on her way back to Italy. Back home.

18

The plane touched down with a bit of a bump which woke Gabriella. This is it, she thought, fifty thousand questions time, and of course telling her parents and brothers about Macario. Gabriella collected her luggage and headed into arrivals where her brothers, Anthony and Mario, were waiting for her.

"Gabriella you look great, that trip certainly agreed with you," Anthony greeted her, as he and Mario gave her a big squeeze. "You look all grown up. Mama and papa are so excited to see you, and by the way, Michael called me and told me about this Macario chap, I have not told mama and papa that he called, we will talk about it later."

Great, thought Gabriella, it's starting already!

When she arrived home, her parents were eagerly waiting for her. "Welcome home Bambino!" Mama and papa virtually threw themselves at Gabriella. "Bella we have missed you so much, let me take your bags," papa exclaimed as he took them from her. "I've made your favourite, meatballs, your room is all clean and ready for you, did you have a good flight?"

"Mama, papa, slow down and let me get in the door! Let me catch my breath then I'll answer your questions." She looked at her brothers.

Gabriella gradually got through answering her parents' questions then sat down for something to eat. The one thing that Gabriella did miss was her mama's cooking. After lunch Gabriella went to her room to unpack. Even though she had the most amazing time away, she was happy to be home. She lay on her bed and drifted off to sleep.

Several hours later, Gabriella woke up to the sound of her phone ringing. It was her best friend Maria.

"Gabby you're home! Why didn't you call me?"

"Maria, I'm sorry, I was going to call you but mama and papa pounced on me as soon as I got in, asked hundreds of questions, I had something to eat and fell asleep. Can you come over? I have so much to tell you!"

"I'm on my way."

Gabriella went down to the kitchen to make herself a drink. It was all quiet in the house and nobody seemed to be around. She looked at the clock. It was seven thirty in the evening. Gabriella found a note left by her parents. *'Gone to Anthony's, papa wants to talk to him about the patisserie won't be long.'*
Oh no, thought Gabriella, please don't say anything about Macario. Then there was a knock at the door.

She opened the door to see Maria with the biggest grin on her face. "Maria, I am so glad to see you, I've missed you so much," Gabriella cried as she flung her arms around Maria, giving her a long hug. "Come in! How are you? Tell me what's been happening since I've been away, how are the gang?"

"I'm fine Gabby, I'm so happy you're home, I've missed you loads! Everyone's good, they are all looking forward to seeing you and hearing about your adventure, but I've got you all to myself first, so tell me, was it everything you expected?"

"Oh Maria it was the best experience of my life, I have learnt so much about the history of the different countries, the people, the different types of food. I was sharing a room with three amazing girls called Martha, Ingrid and Petra, and of course I met Macario!"

"Sounds like you had so much fun, I don't know if I would be brave enough to do it, but at least you have done what you always dreamt of. Now tell me about Macario, what is happening with you two, are you going to stay in touch or was it just a romantic fling?"

"No Maria it definitely was not just a fling, I can't explain it to you because I don't really understand it myself, all I know is that we are meant to be together. So many things happened, there were lots of signs that kept drawing us together. His mother is from Italy and his father is Portuguese, they own lots of restaurants all over the place, they are Catholic and very spiritual people. Macario is building his own restaurant from scratch in Madeira and has offered Michael a job, which he has accepted and he wants me to go and live out there."

"What! Gabby you're not seriously going to are you? You hardly know him, where would you live, what would you do for work? Your parents will hit the roof, look how they reacted when you said you wanted to go traveling."

"I have never been so sure about anything; I know we haven't known each other long, but it's the right thing to do, I just know it."

"Gabby you know I love you very much and only want what's best for you, but this is crazy, he could be some mass murderer! At least get to know him more, go there for holidays, invite him here to meet your parents, just don't do anything hasty. This will break your parents' heart."

"What will break our hearts?"

Gabriella and Maria didn't hear her parents come in. They just looked at each other in horror.

"Hi Mr and Mrs Rossini, I was just leaving. Speak to you later Gabby!"

"Would you like a cup of tea, mama? Papa? How did it go at Anthony's? Did you sort out everything about the patisserie?"

"Gabriella what is going on, what did Maria mean about you breaking our hearts? Are you okay, are you ill?"

No not now, Gabriella thought, this is not going to go down well at all. But no time like the present, I guess.

"Mama, papa there's something I would like to discuss with you, please let me finish before you say anything. When I was traveling I met someone in Madeira, a man that I really like, his name is Macario. He is twenty-two years old, and his mother is from Praiano and his father is Portuguese. They are a Catholic family, they own a chain of restaurants and live in Funchal, Madeira.

When I was in Paris, he came to visit me whilst he was on business there, he had gone to look at a restaurant that his father was interested in buying, and it turned out it was the same restaurant that Michael works in. Macario was so impressed with Michael's food that he has offered him a new position in a restaurant that he is building from scratch, giving Michael total control over what goes on in the kitchen. Macario has also asked me to move out there and I have decided that's what I want to do!"

"Well, Maria was right Gabriella." Mama wiped the tears from her eyes. "You have broken our hearts. Don't you think it was bad enough that you wanted to swan off around Europe? And now you are telling us you want to move to Madeira to be with a man you have known for five minutes. You don't really expect us to agree to this do you?"

"But mama he is really nice, at least meet him, plus Michael will be there to look out for me."

"Gabriella you have been home not even a day and you can't wait to leave again, why you even bothered to come home I don't know." Mama walked out of the room in tears.

"Papa please, it's not like I'm going tomorrow, talk to mama make her understand. I'm not trying to hurt you both, I just want to be happy and I know I will be with Macario."

"Bella you have been away for months, it has been hard for myself and your mama, not knowing if you were safe and now you want to go and be with a boy you don't really know. I'm sorry Bella but we cannot agree to this." Papa went to comfort mama.

Gabriella walked out of the house and went to see her brother, Anthony as it was only a short walk. When Gabriella turned up she was in tears.

"Gabriella what's wrong?" Anthony let her in.

"Mama and papa know about Macario and Madeira. They heard me and Maria talking. Why are they being so difficult about it? I'm not a child anymore."

"But you are in their eyes Gabriella, and as I said to you before, you're their only daughter and they want to look after you and protect you, as we all do. I think that you have been carried away on a romantic notion and not really thought about it. I'm disappointed in Michael; I would have thought he would have talked to you about it."

"Don't blame Michael, he wasn't happy about it but he knew I would go anyway. I can share a place with him and he will look after me, not that I need looking after! If mama and papa met Macario they would see the kind, gentle person that he is, but they won't even give him a chance."

"Gabriella it has come as a shock to them, as it has all of us, mama and papa have really missed you and were so happy that you were coming home. Then you hit them with this. Give it a while and let things blow over."

"I will Anthony, but with or without their blessing, I am going and none of you can stop me." Gabriella stormed out of the house and went back home.

When Gabriella got back she went to her room and called Macario.

"Gabriella are you okay? You sound like you've been crying."

"Oh Macario, it's been awful. My parents overheard me telling my friend about you and moving to Madeira, and now they are really upset and won't talk to me. I was going to leave it for a while to tell them, let them get used to me being back first, but it didn't quite happen the way I wanted it to."

"I'm sorry Gabriella. So you're definitely coming then? I'm sure your parents will come around to the idea. I told my parents and they are looking forward to meeting you. They also think I'm rushing into things but they have never seen me like this before, so they know I'm serious. I have a suggestion, my parents are going to Praiano in a couple of weeks to visit family and I think that would be a good time for them to meet you and your family, and for me to meet your parents and family. What do you think?"

"I think it's a great idea, but trying to convince my parents is another thing, and that's if they are talking to me by then!"

"Don't worry, it will all work out, you'll see. God has put us together because we are meant to be together, your family will see that in time. If they know Michael will be there to watch out for you, they will be fine."

"I don't think so, they are not very happy with him either, they had great hopes that he would come back to Italy and open a restaurant. What a great home coming this has been! I'll speak to you soon Macario."

Gabriella was feeling sad and disappointed that her parents won't be happy for her and respect her wishes. She hoped things may be better in a few days.

***

Gabriella had now been home a week, and things were still not good between her and her parents. Maria called round and they went to the lakes to see their friends. This would be the first time Gabriella had seen them since she had been back.

"Gabriella!" Angelica ran towards her. "You look great, how was Europe? Tell us all about it!"

The gang gathered around as Gabriella told them about all the wonderful places she had been to and the lovely people she had met.

"It sounds amazing; I wish I was brave enough to do it," said Angelica.

"If that's what you want to do, I suggest you do it," Gabriella advised Angelica and all her friends. "It is the most wonderful experience you could ever have, one that I will never forget."

"What about this Marino boy you met?" Marco asked.

"You mean Macario," laughed Gabriella. "He's lovely, you would like him, he's coming to Italy next week with his parents they have family in Praiano. If there's time I'll bring him to meet you all. There is something I want to tell you. Macario has asked me to move to Madeira and I have said yes, it's a long story but as soon as I can, I will be going."

They all looked at Gabriella, not really sure what to say.

Angelica was the first to speak. "But you have only just got back, how can you know someone well enough in a few days to want to pack everything up and move? It's not like you're going to another part of Italy, your moving to another country, and what about your parents? This will really hurt them Gabriella."

"I know we haven't known each other long but it feels right, for both of us. My parents won't even talk about it. I love Macario and he loves me."

"Well if you're sure it's the right thing for you, then, I'm happy for you Gabriella." Angelica gave her a big hug.

After a few hours spent with their friends, Gabriella and Maria walked back to the house.

"Gabby I want to be happy for you, I really do, I just don't want you to make a big mistake, you're young, you have your whole life ahead of you."

"I know you're concerned Maria, and I love you for that, but there really is no need to be, trust me I know what I'm doing. I'll see you tomorrow."

As Gabriella walked into the house, her parents were sitting at the kitchen table looking very sad. Gabriella knew she had to bring the subject up with them again. She took a deep breath and joined them at the table.

"Mama, papa you know how much I love you, and I don't want you to be angry and sad with me, I can understand how you feel, really I can, but I'm not a child anymore. All I ask is that you at least meet Macario. He is coming to Italy next week with his parents and they want to meet you. Please."

"We will meet them Gabriella, maybe his parents can make you see the big mistake you are both making, seeing that you will take no notice of me and your papa."

"Thank you."

Gabriella got up and left the room.

***

The day had finally come. Macario and his parents had arrived in Praiano. Gabriella was excited and nervous at the same time. Excited to see Macario, but nervous meeting his parents and not knowing how her parents were going to react. After a few days of settling in Macario and his parents made the journey to Positano.

Gabriella waited eagerly for them to arrive. Mama made a lasagne and prepared some salad. Anthony and Mario were also there to meet them. Gabriella could see their car approaching the house. Here goes, she thought.

"Macario it's so good to see you!" Gabriella gave him a hug.

"You too. Gabriella, these are my parents."

"Nice to meet you Mr and Mrs Rico. Mama, papa this is Macario and Mr and Mrs Rico."

"Ciao, welcome to our home." They shook hands. "These are two of our sons, Anthony and Mario. I understand you will be meeting our other son, Michael, when he comes to your country!"

"Nice to meet you Mr and Mrs Rossini. Gabriella, you're just as beautiful as Macario described you."

"Please, Mr and Mrs Rico have a seat, my sons will get you a drink. Is caffe americano okay?"

"That's perfect, thank you. Please call us by our first names. I'm Lucia and my husband is Alberto. You have a lovely home. I understand you have your own patisserie?"

"Yes that is correct, we have worked very hard to make it what it is today. People come from nearby towns just for our pastries, isn't that right papa?"

"Yes that's right mama. By the way our names are Rosa and Joe. Gabriella tells us you own a chain of restaurants and that our son, Michael, will be working for you."

"We own a few, always looking to expand," remarked Alberto. Michael will work with Macario, it's his project so it's down to him and Michael. I understand Michael is an excellent chef I'm looking forward to tasting his food."

"Michael is a great chef, his father taught him how to cook at an early age, as is the same with all our children," replied Rosa. "We were hoping that Michael would open his own restaurant in Italy, but I guess that won't happen now."

"I wouldn't rule it out Rosa," assured Lucia, "I'm sure Michael will when the time is right."

"Macario, shall we go for a walk?" asked Gabriella. "Is that okay mama?"

"Yes Bella, be back in an hour for dinner."

"So far so good," Gabriella breathed a sigh of relief. "I have been a bag of nerves; my parents have only just started talking to me so I wasn't sure how they were going to be."

"I think you are worrying too much Gabriella, it will fine, trust, have faith. Michael called me before we left, and I think he is worrying also. I know it's a big move for him and you, but it really will be worth his while. I promise I will make you happy Gabriella."

"I know you will Macario, but what will I do for work? I want to pay my own way; I can share an apartment with Michael."

"Actually, I think my mother may have something for you, something to do with helping children with learning difficulties. She helps out sometimes but they are looking for somebody a bit more permanent, she can explain it better than me."

"Really, that's great. I can't believe that I'm doing this."

"Are you having second thoughts?"

"No not at all, but I must admit it is a bit scary! I think we had better go back to the house and make sure all is peaceful!"

Back at the house, Lucia was helping Rosa with dinner, whilst Alberto and Joe were talking about their restaurants and patisserie with Anthony and Mario. They all seemed to be getting on well which Gabriella and Macario were happy about, especially Gabriella.

After dinner the subject came up about Gabriella moving to Madeira.

"Joe, Rosa, what are your thoughts about Gabriella moving to Madeira?"

"We are not happy about it," replied Rosa. "Gabriella and Macario have known each other a very short time, they are too young to be making this kind of commitment. Gabriella has a secure job here at the patisserie, and she helps students with their English. Maybe if they are still wanting to do this in a few years' time then we can think about it then."

"Mama," Gabriella piped up, "I don't want to wait a few years, I'm ready to do it now."

"How can you be ready Bella, you're still a child?"

"Mama I am not a child, I am twenty years old, a grown woman with a mind of my own, why can't you see that?"

"Gabriella you are still young, too young to be setting up home in a different country by yourself, plus you have no job to go to."

"But I won't be on my own, Michael will be there and I will get work."

"Can I say something?" interrupted Lucia. "Rosa I can understand your concerns, we also think that Macario is rushing into this, but we know our son, and we know that he is a very sensible young man, and would not do anything just on a whim. That's why we are prepared to support him. We have also given him this opportunity to start his own restaurant from scratch because we know, with Michaels help, it will be a success. We believe in our son and the decisions he makes.

We have brought Macario up to be a gentleman and he will be very good to Gabriella and respect her, you have my word on that. As far as Gabriella finding work, I am involved in a small school that helps children with learning difficulties, I am unable to be there all the time due to other commitments, so the school needs someone full time to help. It takes a special kind of person to take such a role on and I think Gabriella would be perfect for it. She would work on a trial basis to start with, then if it all goes well, which I am sure it will, the job will be hers if she wants it. We will look after Gabriella I promise."

"Lucia I appreciate what you are saying, and it is reassuring, but we still feel Gabriella is too young."

Gabriella looked at her parents with such sadness and disappointment, discretely wiping a tear from her eyes.

"We will be in Italy for a few more days Rosa, if you and Joe wish to discuss this any further. We would like to thank you for your kind hospitality, it really is time for us to go. Nice to meet you Anthony, Mario. You have a beautiful daughter, Rosa, Joe, you should be very proud of her."

They all said their goodbyes, Anthony and Mario also left. Macario and Gabriella hung back to say their goodbyes in private.

"I can't believe that they are being so unreasonable," Gabriella sighed. "They treat me like a child. I want to be with you Macario. Maybe I should just pack my bags and leave, it's not like they can stop me."

"I want to be with you too Gabriella but we have to do this the right way, you just getting up and leaving is not the way to do it. I want your parents to be able to trust me, and for them to feel happy knowing that you are in safe hands. Okay, it may take a bit longer then we would like it to be, but at least that way I can come for a few more visits so they can get to know me, and you can come visit me. Give them time to get used to it, we have sprung it on them a bit! By the time you are ready to leave with your parents feeling happier about the situation, the restaurant will be ready and Michael will be there. As I keep saying, trust and it will all come, it's all about divine timing Gabriella, when the time is right it will happen, and without any bad feelings between you and your parents."

"I know you're right Macario, I'll just have to be patient I guess. I will miss you."

Macario and Gabriella said goodbye. Gabriella went back into the house feeling sad, she looked at her parents and said goodnight.

***

Gabriella went back to working in the patisserie, her parents kept Maria on as well. Over several months, Macario came to visit as promised, and Gabriella went to Madeira. They both got to know each other's parents, plus got to know each other better. Gabriella and her parents' relationship was back on track after a rocky few months.

One day, after a long day at the patisserie, Gabriella and her parents returned home to the phone ringing, Gabriella rushed to answer it, it was Mario. His wife, Charlotte, had gone into labour. They were all straight back out the door, picking Anthony up on the way and headed to the hospital.

When they arrived at the hospital they asked a nurse if there was any news. The nurse informed them that it wouldn't be long as Charlotte's labour was quite advanced. After about an hour, Mario appeared.

"Mama, papa you have a grandson. He weighs seven pounds ten ounces and has lots of dark hair, he is just perfect. Charlotte is tired but looks radiant. We have named him Giorgio Joseph."

"Papa they gave him your name!" shrieked an excited Nona. "Can we see him and Charlotte?"

"Of course, come through."

"Bella, Bella!" Mama and papa kissed Charlotte. "You clever girl, thank you for giving us a beautiful grandson."

Gabriella, Anthony and Mario looked at each other and smiled, this was such a happy end to the day.

***

A few months had passed, baby Giorgio was doing really well, Mario and Charlotte were enjoying their son with their other children. Mama and papa were happy; the patisserie was busy as ever. Everything was swimming along nicely, then Gabriella got a call from Macario.

"Gabriella, it's finished, the restaurant is finally ready. We have the official opening next week, I would really love it if you could be here."

"Macario, I am so happy for you, I know how hard you and Michael have worked to get it finished. I wouldn't miss it; I just need to check that my parents can manage without me for a week."

"Actually Gabriella, I was hoping it would be longer than a week. I feel it's time for you to move here now, what do you think?"

"Macario, yes I'm ready. Oh dear, I have to break it to my parents, I am not looking forward to this."

"It will be fine, just you wait and see!" Macario reassured her. "Call me and let me know what happens?"

Before approaching her parents Gabriella called Maria.

"Maria, Macario has just called me, the restaurant is finished and the opening for it is next week and he wants me to be there."

"That's great Gabby, I'm sure we can manage without you at the patisserie for a week."

"Maria he wants me to move there now."

"Oh, I wasn't expecting it to be that soon. Are you sure it's the right time?"

"You know I have been waiting for this day, Macario wanted everything to be just right before I went My parents have accepted him, you like him, my brothers like him, what's there to wait for? I just have to break it to my parents. Maybe I should do it now whilst they're in a good mood!"

"I guess so," sighed an unhappy Maria. "Well good luck, let me know how it goes."

Gabriella put her phone down and approached her parents nervously.

"Mama, papa can I talk to you please?"

"Of course Bella, what's wrong?"

"Macario called, the restaurant is ready and he wants me to be there for the opening next week."

"That's nice Bella, I'm sure we can manage without you for a week."

"Well actually he wants me to move there permanently, not just for the opening." Gabriella held her breath waiting for their reply.

"Bella it's been a long day; we are going to bed now. Sleep well."

Oh no that's not a good sign, thought Gabriella. This is how they always react when they don't want to talk about something. This really has to stop now; I will tell them exactly how I feel in the morning.

Next morning Gabriella was up early; she was getting herself ready for the showdown with her parents. She could hear them coming down the stairs. Here goes, right Gabriella, be strong and tell them as it is.

"Morning mama, papa. Would you like some tea?"

"Yes please Bella."

Okay a good start, Gabriella thought. Now time to tell them.

"Mama, papa first of all I want you to know that I love you very much, I respect you and take on board what you say to me, but sometimes I feel you don't listen to what I say. Now this move that I want to make to Madeira is very important to me."

"Gabriella…"

"No Papa, let me finish please."

"I know you think I'm too young to make my own choices, but I am a grown woman. I love Macario and he loves me. We want to be together and if that means me moving to be with him then that's what I shall do. I hope you can try to understand how I feel; I'm not trying to hurt you I just want to do what is right for me."

"You can go Bella, with our blessing."

"Excuse me!" replied a shocked Gabriella.

"Mama and I have been talking about it, we see how unhappy you are and that's not what we want. We know you're all grown up, but you will always be our little bambino! Go be with Macario, we know he will take care of you, and we are happy knowing that you will be living with your brother."

Gabriella wanted to scream with happiness, will I wake up in a minute and find it was all a dream, she thought to heerself.

"Did you just say I have your blessing to go?" Gabriella stood there, fingers crossed.

"Yes Bella."

"I have to call Macario, thank you, thank you, thank you!" She kissed and hugged her parents.

Gabriella excitedly called Macario to give him the good news and to make plans for her journey. Then she called Michael, who was just as shocked that their parents had agreed to it. Gabriella flopped down on her bed, looked up to the heavens with the biggest smile on her face and thanked God.

***

The following week was busy, getting things ready for Gabriella's move. She met with Maria and they went to the lake to say goodbye to her friends.

"So I guess this is it then?" smiled Angelica. "You're off again, but this time you won't be coming back. We will all miss you Gabriella, please stay in touch and let us know how everything is going."

"Of course I will, you have been my friends for many years and once I'm settled you can all come for a visit. Let's have big group hug, I will miss you all too."

Gabriella waved goodbye and set off back to the house with Maria, who was going to the airport with the rest of the family to say their goodbyes.

Gabriella took as much luggage as she was allowed and the rest of her things would be shipped over. She took one last look around the house, remembering all the wonderful times she had there growing up. She wiped the tears from her eyes and got in the car, taking her last look back.

At the airport, Gabriella checked in her bags and headed off for the departure lounge. This was it.

"Take care Gabriella." Anthony gave her a big hug.

"You will have a great time sis. We will send you regular photos of the children so you can see how they are growing," remarked Mario.

"Maria, I'm going to miss you the most, you are the sister I never had, and you have always been there for me, supporting me even when you thought I was not doing the right things! I love you so much. You can come and visit anytime, and I mean anytime."

"I love you too Gabby, things won't be the same without you here." Maria held on to Gabriella for the longest time.

Mama, Papa, thank you for everything, you are the best parents anyone could ask for. I will keep in regular contact with you, and so will Michael. Come and visit us."

"Oh Bella we will miss you so much, come home and see us soon,"

"I will mama."

There were lots of tears and hugs. Gabriella went through the departure gate, took one last look at her family and waved goodbye.

 Gabriella may have had tears of sadness, but she had a heart full of joy!

ACKNOWLEDGEMENTS

A huge thank you to my daughter Sophie for helping me to shape and perfect this book and for her loving support.

I thank God for the guidance and blessings inspiring me to write this story.

If you enjoyed reading this book, it would be extremely appreciated if you could post a review at the retailer you purchased from.

Lightning Source UK Ltd.
Milton Keynes UK
UKOW05f2327040417
298351UK00001B/76/P

9 781849 149082